# Leo's Cat

Kate Sparrows

Kate Sparrows; kate.sparrows@gmail.com
https://www.facebook.com/kjsparrows

Publisher's Note: This is a work of fiction. Names, characters, places, and incidents are a product of the author's imagination. Locales and public names are sometimes used for atmospheric purposes. Any resemblance to actual people, living or dead, or to businesses, companies, events, institutions, or locales is completely coincidental.

Cover Design: Ariana from Palimpset Designs
Printed by CreateSpace, An Amazon.com Company

Leo's Cat/ Kate Sparrows. -- 1st ed.
ISBN 978-1-943797-00-4

*For you.*

*True love is neither physical, nor romantic. True love is an acceptance of all that is, has been, will be and will not be.*

–Unknown

# CHAPTER ONE

## Leo

Cat was only a few days old when I met her. I remembered looking at that scrunched up little face and thinking I was making the biggest mistake. There was no way that I wanted to be married to something so strange looking. But that's probably what every eight year old thinks of a newborn.

My parents had decided that this was going to be my choice. The problem was, not that they told me, most of the girls my age were already set to be bound to someone. My parents had dropped the proverbial ball a little. That and my father was a bit of a forward thinker. He believed in a long forgotten thing of love. Well, marrying for love.

These days, people were more advanced. Albeit there were less of us and scatter in small parts of the still inhabitable world. By the time I'd graduate, I would learn of the ecological impacts the peoples of the past made and the genetic research done ages ago that molded our race today. But all I knew as a young boy was that I could turn into animals. My parents could turn into animals, and everyone else I knew as well. I knew that I would have a Coming-of-Age ceremony when I was sixteen, and get presents. I would one day have a wedding and be bound to someone who'd have my litter.

Litters. That was a strange concept, but yet everyone wanted to have them. I wasn't part of a litter and neither was this tiny baby girl. We were both only children. But putting a litter inside someone was the ultimate goal of binding. It meant having more than two children and what resulted where better shifters. They seemed to transform the fastest, and earliest, and into the most variety of animal species. They also seem smarter, but that might have been because they were favored in the communities. In reality, the latter was false but the key in the belief was to rebuild the worldly population.

But my innocent eyes looked down at that pink face and wondered if she was going to be my *One*. There were five girls, all years younger than me, whom my parents lined up for me to choose. They wanted the decision to be mine, unlike the arrangement every other child went through. At the time I didn't know how kind, or how cruel, that was.

"Mama, can I have her?" My voice finally showed up. It was strange to feel such wrinkly skin, but even more to have a little hand wrap around my finger. It was almost like she was picking me too.

"What's her name?"

The lady holding the baby smiled. "Her name's Cat."

# CHAPTER TWO

# *Leo*

I knocked on the door and tried to wait. Mom said I had to start doing this alone. One day Cat was going to be my wife and I'd have to take care of her. I hadn't realized those years ago in the hospital that it would start right now.

Her father opened the door. "Oh, Leo! You here for Cat?"

I nodded. I hated her name. At least, I did now. Johnny teased me about us both being felines and would purr whenever I walked by. Johnny was a jerk though. I felt bad for Ciera who was going to be bound to him. But why did they have to name her "Cat"?

And it was as if on cue. Her little face poked around her father's leg after she ran into him. It was never the walking, well, running, part that got Cat. It was the stopping. Once she got started on our walks, she didn't stop until those stubby legs gave out and I'd have to carry her home. I had gotten wiser and knew when to loop back towards her house.

"Hair?" She smiled. It was the cutest and silliest thing ever with her semi-toothy grin. It looked like my four-year-old fiancé had lost another tooth since my last visit.

I smiled as she waddled over and hugged my leg. Her flaxen hair was always so soft, and today it was in pigtails. "It's very pretty. Did your mama braid it?"

I know she did, but I can't be mean to Cat. It's hard to when she's always smiling at me. She nods and I hold her hand.

"She's been talking about ducks all morning. She wants to show you them, but it might be too far to walk to the pond." I know of the pond he's talking about. It is too far for our walks. Cat hasn't had her first transformation yet, so turning into something else to get us there is out of the question. And I don't think I'm that strong enough to carry her the whole way there and back.

"How about we go look at flowers?" I ask her while she slowly takes the steps down, one at a time. Her grin's huge as she makes the last one. I doubt she really cares what we go see. I think it's more of spending time with me, seeing as I'm only allowed weekly visits. We used to try two but it was so hard with school and her naps, and I wanted to play on the soccer team with my friends.

I held her hand as we walked. Cat tried to tell me all her stories from the past week. There was a lot of stories there, just not a whole lot of words. But that was another thing we were doing. I'd try to see how many words I could teach her with things I pointed out. She learned "car", even if it was just for that day. Listening to her try to pronounce it for the first, and second, time was adorable. Her face would get a little red when she got flustered because it didn't sound right to her. Or as she said – *"Not like Leo."*

I tell her about my day, how school is going, and soccer. I know she doesn't understand yet. She has a pre-school group once a week to play and learn little kid things, but it's not the same. And it's hard to talk about things from school anyways. She was going to just be starting kindergarten and I was in middle school, where we were learning algebra and what sex was. And one day, I knew I was going to have sex with Cat. It was hard not to think of her like a little baby and the whole thing being gross. But she was mine and I was pretty sure I loved her, in some way.

CHAPTER THREE

# Leo

I pushed her hard. Of all the days that I could have taken her to the park, why did it have to be today? It always ended up turning into whatever Cat wanted to do. I knew that, just like I knew I had to be nice and keep my wife-to-be happy. But why today? Today was *my* day. It was the only day of the year that should be all about me and my parents made me go see her, which landed us here and on the swings.

All I had wanted for my fourteenth birthday was a superhero cake and a skateboard. But instead, everyone's forgotten and expects me to babysit.

I shove Cat again, forcing her to swing higher. In my anger, I want to make her cry but all she does is laugh and beg me to do it again. Why can't she just cry and make me take her home? I don't even want to be around her.

"Leo, push!"

I had let her swing for a while and she wasn't flying up as high or as fast.

"Cat, it's time to go home." If she wasn't going to ask, then I would tell her. Maybe I'd still have time to run down to Elmer's and get a birthday cake flavored ice cream cone. They were the best with little chunks of birthday cake and ribbons of frosting in the ice cream. Plus, the old guy would dip the top in chocolate or butterscotch if you wanted before rolling the scoop in rainbow sprinkles. And after the way things were going, I needed something to redeem the day.

I caught glimpses of a pout on her little face as she swung by. "No. Push!"

Reaching out, I slowed the swing to a stop only to speed her whining. "Leo, push. Pwease!" She tried to squirm away from my hands so she couldn't be taken out of the little kids' swing.

"Cat, I said we are going home *now*."

It was a battle to get her legs out of the holes. Why was she being so stubborn? Why today? I always did what she wanted. Why couldn't she just do one thing I wanted?

I managed to get her out but the moment her feet hit the ground, she took off running. "Cat, get back here!"

She was faster than I'd like to admit. What made it worse was that she could transform now. I watched her shift into a fox and take off. I had to catch her soon. She could weasel out at the small gap in the fence along the woods or crawl under the small bathroom building or any half dozen other places that I was too big to get at her. And that's where it looked like she was heading – the bathrooms.

Shifting to a fox, myself, it took less than two heartbeat to catch up to her short legs. I grabbed her by the scruff of her neck, hearing the disgruntled whines as she tried to wiggle free. Cat was even more annoying as a fox when she was upset and pouting.

*"Leo, down!"*

I shake my head as I head out of the park. There's no way I'm caving today. Birthday cake ice cream is set in stone with the stunt she pulled. If I have to carry her back and shove her in a shoe box, then so be it.

*"Leo, you be a meanie!"* She kept shouting at me in her whiny fox talk. Not once did she stop her complaining as we walked the mile back to her house. Not once did she ever stop to think about anyone but herself, especially what day it was. She never cared that

it was a day she'd get cake, which she loved being able to get it twice a year – on her birthday and mine.

I turned back on her doorstep, keeping my grip on her. Cat tried to wiggle out of my human fingers but I moved to hold her like a baby in my arms. "I'm going to put you in a box if you don't stop, Cat. Gosh, can't you just... ugh!"

She barked at me as the door opened. Here I thought her whining was the worse. That little yip was earsplitting. I tell her to stop it as I walk into her house and freeze. It's full of people, and all their eyes are on us. Cat stopped squirming as my mom brought out a cake.

"Happy Birthday, Leo!" They all cheered.

*They remembered...*

Cat's mom came to take her from me and allowed her to turn back. "Good job, sweetie. You kept him away just long enough." I managed to catch her hushed words and it kind of started to make sense. The way my parents acted like it was just another day. The way Cat was more a whiny kid.

"Sweetie, why don't you go wish Leo a happy birthday?"

I watched as her mom gave her a little nudge. Timidly, she walked over and I crouched to be at her level. Cat bumped into me in her attempt at a hug and pushed me back on my butt. People were starting to laugh but, before I could get angry over that, their laughter turned into ah's.

Cat had leaned up to kiss my cheek. "Happy bwirthday, Leo. I wuv you."

And with the missing tooth grin on her face, I couldn't help but smile back. "Thanks, Cat." Giving her a peck on the cheek only turned her red as a beet.

I ran-walked over and saw the superheroes on the cake. As everyone sang, I leaned in and blew out my candles. It was so hard to wish for just one thing. There was so much I wanted and so much I thought I needed. Instead I made a wish for the cutie that was eying my cake. I watched her over the candle flames as I had blew them out.

*Make Cat be a sexy wife with big boobs... and lots of duct tape for when she starts whining.*

CHAPTER FOUR

#

"Cat!"

I waved at Mae and scooted over so she could sit by
me. She was my first and best friend at school. The
first few years were fun and I thought I was going to
love school, but then the binding thing started. By the
fourth grade, I was more of an outcast. All the other
kids were just starting to pair up and figure out if they
liked the person their parents arranged for them. I was
the only one who never had to worry. I had Leo.

He was always there for as long as I could
remember. The thing was, he was always my brother in
my mind. Leo was there when I took my first steps and
he helped me learn to ride a bicycle. We went

swimming at the community pool every week in the summers. He even helped me with my homework.

Leo still felt like my brother, even though everyone kept reminding me that he'd become my lover one day. And it didn't help to know that my Coming-of-Age ceremony was happening in a few short months. It was hard to believe that I was going to be sixteen already, which meant that Leo was already twenty-four.

I sighed as Mae chatted about her chemistry lab. Not because of her story, which seemed to be the same every day, but because my mind was on Leo again.

"You thinking about your stud?"

That got my attention. "No," I said defensively, my face turning deep red.

She just laughed, almost choking on her gum. "Why not? Leo's totally a hottie."

I groaned. It wasn't like I hadn't heard it before, and not just from Mae. If Leo wasn't Leo, she'd be right. His body was great and he had a sexy voice. That is, if Leo wasn't my Leo. "Mae, he's like my brother. He saw me in diapers. Hell, he changed my diapers."

"So? Just means he loves you." That was a strange thought. Leo loved me? "I bet he's a sex god."

I almost choked on my sandwich. "Mae!" She just laughed at me.

"What?" She shrugged.

"You know what." I shook my head, trying to get that image out of my head. I couldn't be thinking about

Leo naked. It was just... wrong. But I couldn't stop wondering what he looked like with his briefs off.

# CHAPTER FIVE

"Ugh, why do I need to know this?"

Mae giggles. It must be at how different Leo and I are. He always has to force me to do my History homework. I hate the subject.

"Because it's important."

I know he's standing over me, probably with his hands crossed in front of his chest and looking like a scolding parent. Just like I know Mae only insists on studying at my house because she knows Leo will be here and she can ogle him.

"But Leo, this happened so long ago that it's practically ancient history. It *is* ancient history." I get off my stomach and sit to look at him. "They shouldn't be teaching us why some stupid scientist thought splitting DNA was the only way to save the world. I bet he just wanted to be a batman."

He groans. "Batman is not a half-bat half-man person, Cat. He's a superhero. One of the best the ancient people came up with." Leo goes to flop on the couch with some comic book. "A lot better than these superheroes that just say not to kill anything because it could be your brother. Seriously, Captain Conscious?"

I really have no clue what Leo's talking about. Comics are a guy thing and the ones he reads are more for the extreme nerds. And no matter how many times he tries, I will never like those stories.

"Whatever." I roll my eyes and stare at my textbook. "I still don't get why we can't learn about some wars or stuff. That happened back them too."

"But this actually affects us." Oh great, Mae's chiming up now and taking Leo's side. It's times like these that her crush on him gets really annoying. "Because of what these guys thought about one of these apocalypses or whatever that Sixth Extinction thing was, they changed us. They put animal DNAs in people, thinking we'd be able to change into anything to survive."

"Yea, and that failed on them. Didn't it?" I grab my notebook and try to scribble down enough of what they were saying for this two page essay. I knew that at least eighty percent of the world population was wiped out after the extinction and the surviving groups were really spread out. That's what caused this bonding thing, and why I was promised to Leo before I even knew how to projectile vomit his face.

"Okay, so the global warming and the ice age weren't as bad as they thought and nuclear war really didn't happen and the biodiversity thingy really wasn't that big of an issue... but it's important. Right, Leo?"

I glare at him as he nods. Of course, his nose is deep in his comic book and he ignores me.

"Sure, some crazy person gets an idea and screws up the whole world. Let's force centuries of kids to learn out the lunatic and say it all was to help us!"

"Cat, it's not all that. You have to remember that they were a different race back then. They had different beliefs and customs. Even their language was a little different back then." Leo peeps up again. "They're just trying to make sure you know why you are the way you are; which, right now, is an annoying little pipsqueak."

That did it. "I'm a what!?"

I tackle him on the couch, going for all his ticklish spots. I only get him to laugh a couple times before he turns the tables and has me pinned to the couch.

"A pipsqueak." He says it again and I try to wiggle free. It's not fair that he's bigger than me and he's using it against me.

I say the only thing that I know bothers him. "Let me go you old man!"

Leo does and I have to say that I am surprised. But then a devilish look grows on his face. He hasn't moved off me yet, and now I know why. He starts tickling me and I'm laughing so hard that I can't breathe. I need to get him off me and the only thing I can think of is to be bigger than him.

I transform into a polar bear and Leo rolls off me. He lands with a thud on the floor, and Mae's laughing her head off at us. I glare at her but she knows I wouldn't maul her, even though that's the look I'm trying to go for. The only glare really working right now is the one from Leo.

"Cat, turn back or I'll tell your parents you were trying to break the couch."

I grumble and give in. What's the use of being able to transform when all it does is get you in trouble? I can't help but sit on the couch, pouting.

"You're a meanie, Leo."

He laughs and moves to sit next to me. I want to attack him again because of his smug look, but I know it'll just end up with me begging for mercy.

"Would a meanie be helping you and your friend with their homework?" I don't say anything when he tries to prove he's right by being the logical one. Leo leans in and I just stare straight ahead trying to ignore him. "If you finish everything else, I'll help you write the essay later when Mae goes home," he whispers.

That's the best deal I'm probably ever going to get. I know Leo would never write the stupid thing for me. I nod glumly and go back to lie on the floor to do my math and science homework. I love math, with all those equations and stuff. Math always made sense.

# CHAPTER SIX

# Cat

"It's going to be fine, sweetheart." He kisses my forehead. "I'll be there, so it won't be so bad."

I roll my eyes. As if that made the whole ceremony better. I have to wear a dress. A dress! And I have to make vows then announce the name of my mate, who had claimed me. It was going to be embarrassing. What's worse, my parents invited the whole family, mine and Leo's, plus my friends had threatened to stop by.

"Can't you just shoot me now? It's going to be awful." I groan and slide another dress over on the rack. How Leo ended up here, at the department store helping me pick out a dress, I'll never know. I sighed and slide over another neon colored mess.

"We could skip," I say, hopeful, as I turn. "It's going to be boring and you already sat through your own boring one. Please, Leo." I smile up at him, hoping to get him to give in. I had managed to get him to crack in the past. He was probably debating it too. I could tell from that look that he was thinking something over.

He reaches past me and pulls something off a rack. Stepping back, he holds the soft rose dress against my body. "I think you should wear this." He smiles. "Why don't you go try it on, sweetheart?"

I groan and snatch it from his hands. He had been thinking alright. Thinking what would look good on me. I hear him chuckle as I slipped into the fitting room to try it on. And the dress wasn't that bad on me. It came to just above my knees and was so soft. I turned around to see myself from the back and smiled that none of my tan lines really showed. It shouldn't have surprised me that Leo picked something my parents would approve as "age appropriate" and yet something that had skin showing.

I tugged up the sweetheart neckline and pushed back the curtain so he could see. "Well?" I watched as his eyes traveled down my body and then slowly back up. He looked hungry, and it was a look that seemed to be coming out a lot more lately. At first it gave me the shivers, but now I sorta accepted it.

Leo stepped closer, resting his arms around my waist. "Beautiful." He smiled and glanced down at the dress again. His hand slid down a little to the hem as he kissed me. "Perfect." Leo smiles and gently pushes me back into the fitting room.

His lips move down to my neck as his fingers skim over my skin. I bite my lip to keep quiet as his hands roam a little further up. I had no idea why he was doing this, and it felt so weird. What if someone came by and saw us? This couldn't be right. Could it?

I panicked a little when he pushed me up against the wall and his fingers reached the bottom of my panties. It was hard to tell if he moaned or groaned, but Leo back away a little. The hunger sparkled in his eyes. For what seemed like an eternity, neither of us said a word.

"I can't wait until your mine," Leo says softly. His eyes trail slowly over me one last time before he sighs and pulls the curtain closed.

I stand there, stunned. What had just happened? He had gone further than any other time. Up until now, he had just kissed me and it seemed flirty. This, that look, it felt different and I couldn't help but think it was because of this ceremony. It made me even more nervous and my hands shook a little as I unzipped the back

I brush back his hair from his eyes as he gazes up at me from my lap. I was so happy that he took me out today. The weather was perfect for a picnic. And it seemed like things between us were even better since my Coming-of-Age ceremony. Leo seemed more relaxed, more like his normal self. The only thing that seemed to change was that I got to sleep over at his apartment in town on the weekends and he kept insisting that I wear more dresses.

"So what do you want to do tonight?"

I smile down and ponder it. "Well, we could rent a movie. We haven't stayed in for a while." Usually our nights consisted of going out to dinner and, lately, dancing. Really anything that kept us close to each other. "We could snuggle on the couch and you can try to catch popcorn kernels that I toss at you," I tease.

He rolls his eyes and sits up. "So you don't want to head downtown? It's supposed to be a clear night. We could sit outside. I was thinking maybe that little café on the corner of Mason Ave."

"What if I don't want to share you with anyone?" I pout, not that I was proud of it. A blind person could even see the affect he had on people, the girls especially.

Leo chuckled and kissed me softly. "Okay, sweetheart, we'll stay in tonight." He beams that smile at me. "Do you want to help me in the kitchen or should I cook and have it ready for when you come over?"

That was Leo, always trying his best to please. "Can I watch you cook?" I suggest. It was nice sometimes to just sit back and watch him work. The way he was so focused and how his body moved. It was like watching a painter work a canvas or a fly-fisherman gracefully wipe the line back and forth. Plus it was the only time I had around him to think. I knew I was as bound to him as possible without the ceremony, but I couldn't shake thinking of Leo as my brother. He was always there, and still was for me.

"And I need help with math."

"Math?" He chuckles. "I thought you were a wiz in math."

I roll my eyes. "I *am*, but we're starting advanced stuff and you know I hate it." I sigh. It wasn't exactly the truth. Out of all my subjects, math was my best one. It was just my other weakness, besides watching Leo. I could get so focused on one little part of the problem and spend an hour trying to decipher it, just to have him point out I'm supposed to find X. "And I have history stuff too. I have to write about the ancients and the technology boom that led to us changelings."

He sighs and wraps his arms around me. "Okay, how about we try to do that history stuff before dinner and the movie. Then save math for right before bed? I know you can zoom through that."

Leo kisses me again, and I knew he was right. If nothing else, I'd have time in the morning before class to finish it. "As long as you promise to check my answers."

He didn't promise anything. He just kisses me again and, for a moment, I forget what we had been talking about.

"How about I clean up and you fly home to pack for tonight?" He says softly. There was just part of me that wanted to melt from that smile.

CHAPTER EIGHT

# Cat

I was finally getting a good rhythm going. I figured that maybe I should work on my land animal modes. Lately I had been favoring sparrows and hawks. I was beginning to worry that I'd never be able to make a less obvious escape, if my life depended on it.

As kids, Leo had always managed to catch me. He'd joke and taunt me into his little game. Of course, if that didn't work, he'd get me angry or upset and chase after me when I tried to get away. Back then I had an obsession with foxes. I'd transform into a sleek vixen, dashing under fallen trees in the woods and through brooks. Somehow he'd always be on my heels or followed my scent so well that I wondered if he stuck me with a tracker. I had even started to get crafty by transforming mid-chase into a mouse or sparrow, hoping to throw him off, but he'd always pounce on me. I was never fast enough to escape. Then again, Leo played dirty.

I rounded the path around the lake. The few chirping birds and the sound of my feet pounding the asphalt were my music. Running wasn't just vital to us, but for me it was therapeutic. From the corner of my eye, I noticed a large something heading straight for me. I may have shrieked, embarrassingly, and tripped over my feet, landing on my ass.

A laugh and a sturdy hand were there to help me up. "I thought you heard me. I was calling your name."

"I was in the zone." I glare up at Leo's amused face.

"I see that, sweetheart."

He helped me up and brushed off my backside. My hands shooed him away. Any excuse to touch me. "You're incorrigible."

Leo kisses me, ending that train of thought and evaporating some of the anger. "So, how'd you find me?" I ask as we started to walk the rest of the trail.

"Mae told me. Well, I stopped by your house and your mom said you were out with friends." I'm not sure why I was surprised. Mom thought if I wasn't with Leo that I was always with friends. Friends being one, Mae. It wasn't like I was a rebellious teen out sleeping around and ruining my life and prospects of being bound to a mate. And Leo had managed to break Mae into giving him her number, "just in case". He had winked when he told me that one. "So why aren't you?"

"Because I was never going to hang out with her. I felt like a run." As if my workout clothes hadn't made that obvious. It wasn't like I was dressed for the mall or something. "Were you looking for me for something?"

He shook his head. *What was up with that?*

"You could have saved yourself some trouble and called my cell."

"Would you have called me back, sweetheart?" He glances at me sideways. I know he's questioning me and my actions.

"Of course!" It was the truth. Why wouldn't I have?

"But you don't run with your phone," he stated matter-of-factly. As if he would know all my habits. But there was a knowing look as he wink at me. "I tried."

That flabbergasted me even more. "Okay... so what did you want?"

"Nothing." He smiled.

I could sense there was something more to it than that. This wasn't the first time he tagged along. I couldn't think of a single day without Leo. I wasn't sure how I felt about this newfound clinginess. But that was the only thing that made sense. He was keeping tabs on me.

# CHAPTER NINE

# Cat

I groan as my mom pulled out yet another version of white dress. We had been at this all morning. I wanted to just plop back down in my chair and let her just pick. It didn't really matter than much to me because I knew Leo was just going to be thrilled it was finally happening.

"Cat, don't you get an attitude. This is all that's left to do for the wedding. I got the elder to do the ceremony and everything's set. Now just pick out a dress and it's as good as done."

She smiled sweetly. Almost too sweetly, as if there was something she wasn't telling me. I look at the new additions to the rack of dresses to try on. They all looked the same at this point. I ran my hand over them, feeling the differences in fabrics. A noise in the back of my head told me which ones Leo would love. We had enough make-out moments that I knew which textures made it harder for him to move away. I should want to keep him in those moments for our wedding, right?

The rack of choices kept growing. It was looking like this would be an all day ordeal. Mom pulled one out of the sea of white short dresses. "Cat, come on. Get started trying these on!"

I stepped back and thought about taking the dress in her hands. I knew Leo loved me in short dresses. It showed off more skin and gave his fingers more space to roam. But did I really want that on my wedding day? It wasn't like I was trying to go against Leo and the whole binding thing. I wanted this day to stand out, to be special.

"I want a long dress," I say as firmly as I could muster. It was hard to stand up when I was being pulled under up short garments and my mom.

I spotted one pearly dress in the window. Sweetheart neckline. Ruched and light sparkly beaded bodice. Then beautiful draped, flowing floor length fabric. That was my dress. It was perfect for what would be the biggest day of my life and seeing it, I just knew Leo would love it.

# CHAPTER TEN

# *Cat*

I yawn and climb out of the tangle of sheets and Leo's arms. It had been like this almost every night. Our wedding was only a couple months away now, and with each passing day my parents seemed more lax about our boundaries. I was spending so many nights at his apartment that I was starting to forget what my own bed felt like. And then on the days I stayed home, Leo would crawl under the sheets with me.

Half in a daze, I head for the kitchen. It was the same old routine at Leo's. Wake up. Pour glass of milk. Get coffee started. Drink milk. Pop in toast. Wake him up. It only varied a little depending if I had to dash off to school or not. But we always had a few moments together before going our separate ways.

I start to head back to wake him when I am pushed up against the wall. Leo was hungry today, and not just for food. I came to learn quickly what "morning wood" felt like pressed against my body. However, I knew this time it wasn't just going to be some flirty comment or joke.

His lips were attacking my neck, marking me with his affections. One hand had already slipped underneath my pajama top while the other was at my hip, pulling me closer. I gasped and gripped the front of his grey t-shirt as he cupped my breast.

I could feel his lips turn up into a smile against my skin. Every instinct was telling me to let go. To let out the moan I tried so desperately to keep in, and let him know I was getting aroused. To let myself be turned on and to forget seeing Leo as my brother.

Leo was hard as he rocked against me. He had no problems letting out a low moan that curled in primal lust in the back of his throat. Meanwhile, all I could do was hang on and wait for it to be over. Leo would never let it go too far, even if this was further than last time.

It was a conflicted groan that escaped to the sound of toast popping up. Even the coffee machine had sputtered into silence. His eyes were closed as he rested his forehead against mine.

"I can't wait until I'm yours, sweetheart."

CHAPTER ELEVEN

# Cat

I pace my bedroom. I knew I had to tell Leo. He would understand. Mae wouldn't and I'm not even sure my parents would. But Leo would. He had to or the rest of my life would be miserable.

Yesterday at lunch I had brought up how I wasn't sure I wanted to have a litter. Mae only felt the need to remind me how ridiculous I was. My mate was a stud, and it could be worse. Cindy was the girl in our grade that she always seemed to compare every situation to. She was bound almost a year ago and it was going horribly. Her husband and Cindy basically were strangers. They had tried to make it work but, after a few months and no litter or baby, they realized they had nothing in common to keep a relationship going. Somehow they managed to forget about that long enough to have a boy a couple months ago. In fact, Mae said her husband was pushing again for more, thinking they'd just do it that way and call it a litter.

But Mae had looked at me like I was a freak. In time, I'm sure Leo would accept that part but I doubt he'd take the kicker so well. Guys were always told early on about the binding thing and how it would be unlimited sex for life afterwards. For everyone but Leo, it was a rough wait of merely twenty years. Leo was pushing thirty. He told me all of his friends were married and had kids. He claimed it never bothered him about us because he got to pick his wife and I was worth the wait. To admit I was petrified and didn't want a litter was one thing. To admit I never wanted to have sex would kill him... kill us.

Any minute now he was going to get here, and I still had no idea how or if I was going to tell him. No sooner had I thought this and the doorbell rang. I knew who it was and I should have bolted downstairs to try to beat my parents to the door, but I was too nervous. Somehow I had to make it through dinner, keeping in this secret. It hadn't really bothered me until I realized how wrong it was for me to feel like this. Somewhere along the way, I must have gotten broken, and now Leo was going to pay for it.

I headed downstairs, pausing halfway down to listen in. It seems like he brought a cheesecake for dessert. Crap! Couldn't he, just once, not be perfect and wonderful? They were talking about the wedding and where it was all going to be. I heard him say how excited he was, that he couldn't wait to have me all to himself. Would he still want me when he knew?

"There she is!" Leo smiled and scooped me up in his arms when I reached the bottom of the stairs.

I couldn't help but laugh at how ridiculous he was while he spun me around. "Yea, a whole nine hours." I roll my eyes as he sets me down.

"Feels longer, sweetheart." He kisses me and takes my hand as we head to the dining room to enjoy my mom's lasagna. She always seems to make something a little better when he's over for dinner, like she really needs to try wooing Leo into marrying me. There's no way he could want me more, and it was slightly frightening.

My parents decide that they were going to pop in a movie and asked if we wanted to join them. I was so content, my tummy happy with the cheesecake, that I would have agreed to anything. I smiled and rested my head on Leo's shoulder as he rubbed my arm. He quite smoothly declined and somehow got the OK to head upstairs with me. I was pretty use I heard "massage" in there and that was good enough for me. Getting one from Leo was fan-tastic! Giving him one was funny, with him trying to sniffle his noises and wiggling when I'd hit a ticklish spot.

"Thank god." He shook his head, closing my bedroom door. "I'm pretty sure your mom's in love with me now. Maybe I shouldn't have brought the cheesecake."

"Hey, don't you dare say that! That cheesecake was good." I rub my stomach a little for emphasis.

"You know what else tastes good?" Leo smirked and walked over to me, wrapping his arms around my waist. When I shook my head, his smile grew. "You."

He kisses me and I just melt into him. My mind had turned off as he slowly moved in direction of my bed. It wasn't until I felt it against the back of my legs did I start to panic. Was I ready for this next step? We never made-out on a bed before. Just morning and night kisses.

"Leo, do you want to put a litter inside me?" It blurts out.

A screeching halt doesn't even begin to describe what happened. Leo looked like a deer caught in the headlights. I almost felt bad for asking, but I knew it eat me alive if I didn't know now.

"Um, sure... of course I do." He must have seen my face fall. "Why, don't you want me to?"

"I do, but I..." I couldn't look at him. I was scared of what I would see. "I don't think I want kids. They're going to change everything and I don't anything to change. I want you to be you and me to be me, and us to just be like this forever."

He gently brushed his thumb over my cheek and kissed me. "We'll still be the same. I promise."

"I'm scared, Leo. I... I don't think I can do." I try to blink away a few of the tears that started puddle in my eyes.

"Shh." He pulls me closer into his arms. I knew he was trying to reassure me, but I couldn't see that when the whole dam was breaking. "I'll be right next to you the whole time. It'll be alright, sweetheart. We'll get through-"

"I don't want to have sex with you." I felt him freeze. There was no warmth anymore and he was barely even moving. If my head wasn't near his heart, I would have thought he died. But maybe he did. "I mean, I..."

Leo let me go. I was stupid enough to look at his face and he was devastated. He didn't understand. Oh God, he didn't understand. Nothing I thought was right, and nothing coming out of my mouth made anything better.

"Leo, I don't want to have sex at all. I want to have sex with you! I just... I don't want to... do it."

A glint on his face makes my voice catch in my throat. *Oh, no! Please don't cry, Leo. Please... no.* I had never seen him cry, not once. I thought I knew what would happen, but I had no idea it would be like this. I have to fix this. I don't want him to cry because it's killing me to watch one tear after another run down his face that ever showed me love. And now, it was showing nothing but hurt. Hurt that I caused.

I reach out to him. I'll do it. I'll do it all, even if I don't want it. I'll get through it. Just... "Leo," the word comes out strangled and quiet.

He just steps back, shaking his head. His eyes search mine trying to find some hope and praying this was a sick joke, I know it. I take a step closer and be bolts. I hear the front door slam a moment later and I know. I lost him. I lost the only man who loved me. The only man I ever loved. All because I couldn't stop being the scared little girl he always rescued. All because I couldn't realize sooner how deeply I loved him and how nothing else mattered. I'd have sex with him every night. I'd have his litter and his kids. I just wanted him, and he was enough.

My rock was gone and I had nothing to keep me together anymore. My legs gave out moments before my parents peeked in. I knew they were going to ask what happened, but I was too empty inside to do anything but cry in their arms. Leo had my heart, he always did, and now it was ripped out of me.

# CHAPTER TWELVE

# Cat

I didn't leave the house. I barely left my room. All I did was try calling and texting him. I had to get him back. I loved him too much to lose him. It had been nearly a week, and I hadn't seen Leo once. And we had never gone a day before without each other! I was losing it.

My parents knew what happened, what I had said. They were just as upset as Leo, in their own way. Dad got angry and tried to pound into my head what our race did now. There were traditions. I had thought they were so liberal and forward thinking. They let their newborn daughter be paired up with a boy almost halfway done with school.

Mom was the worst. She cried almost as much as I did. I knew she blamed herself. She was the only one to listen to me, to try to understand my fears. And as the days ticked away with no signs of Leo, she started to take my side more and help us both understand. She talked my dad down and into listening. I was getting my parents back slowly, and I desperately needed their support, but Leo was as close to me as the Sun was to Pluto. And I couldn't take it anymore.

I knew I loved him. Nothing else mattered, and I knew I was a fool for taking love so lightly. I had taken Leo for granted. I had to get him back.

"Mom, I'm going to try and talk to him," I called as I headed out of the house. I had tried to stop by one other time, but I missed him. It seemed like he was working more hours just to avoid me, and I had no idea if that was true or just something my mind made up to make me feel worse. But it was probably a good thing, because I had shown up with puffy red eyes, snotty nose and looked so ugly from crying that I'd probably have scared him away for good, if I didn't scare him to death.

I transformed into a sparrow and flew across town to his apartment. I was slightly relieved to see a light on, but at the same time nervous as hell. That meant I was going to have to figure out what to say, and last time that didn't go well at all. I landed on his doormat and knocked, once I had hands again. I waited for him to come to the door, or at least for any sign of him. I figured that there would at least be a shadow movement in the peephole, but there wasn't even that. How could he be avoiding me if he didn't even know it was me? I stepped off the doormat, towards his living room window. The binds were open a bit and I could see him inside on the couch. He was sitting there, not moving. *Oh my god!*

I couldn't look away even though I wanted to. I stared in horror as some brunette jerked off my mate. I could see Leo's eyes rolling back before he closed them and his mouth hung open. I wanted to do something to make it stop, to make him see me, to make him hurt as much as he was hurting me now. I wanted to be the only one to see him, to touch him, to give him the pleasure that made that look on his face.

Leo must have been coming off the high of that messy orgasm because his head started to fall forward again and his eyes were opening. They found me in an instant, as if they were trained to locate me at all times. I couldn't stop the tears flowing down my face, but I didn't move to brush any of them away. He deserved to see how much he just hurt me and I deserved it after what I said.

It looked like he was getting up but, for what, I'd never know. I wasn't going to give him a chance to lie to me, to make me feel like it was my fault, to try to pretend it never happened or wasn't what I was thinking. I bolted and must have broken the sound barrier. I never remembered the flight home to be so quick, but then I had extra emotions fueling me.

My parents had been watching something on the television was I stumbled in. My vision was so blurry that I had no idea how I managed to find my way home.

"Cat!"

I felt my mom's embrace and buried my face into her shoulder to cry. "Cat, honey, what's wrong?" She rubbed my back, trying to soothe me but there wasn't anything in the world that could.

"L-Leo." I couldn't believe how shaky and broken my own voice felt. My dad turned off the television and walked over, hearing who it was about. No doubt he was wondering how bad he was going to beat Leo's ass for putting me in such a state. My mom tried to ease more out of me, to get me to talk and tell them what was wrong.

"H-he... he was with... someone else." I try to get the images out of my head, but they keep coming back to taunt me. To prove I couldn't pleasure him like that, that I wasn't good enough. "He and a girl... she was touching him and... she jerked him off and..." Leo's face played over and over as it changed. I knew exactly when it happened to him. I could only imagine the sounds that escaped him. And I hated myself for it all.

A frantic knock at the door made me jump. I could hear his voice calling for me. It seemed like we were all at a standstill inside. "I don't want to see him," I whispered. It was all the strength that I had left.

My mom helped me upstairs and into bed while my dad answered the door. He tried to keep his voice down, but I could hear them fighting as I cried into my pillow and listened to my mom's hum, trying to relax me. But there was nothing. Not anymore.

# CHAPTER THIRTEEN

# Leo

Her parents invited me over. I knew it wasn't for anything good. Without them saying, I knew it was about the other night I had made a horrible judgment call. And now I knew I lost the only girl I ever really loved.

"What the hell? You were supposed to be there for her, to love her and you what? Screw some other chick? We thought you were better than that. We thought you'd deserve our daughter."

Her father's words sting, but I know he's right. Cat deserved more than what I gave her. "There was no excuse for what I did," I say quietly, trying to keep eye contact. I have to let them see how sorry I really am, that I'm not trying to get out of this, and I have to see any glimmer of hope that they'd let me go through with this wedding. I don't want to lose Cat, and definitely not over a mistake.

Amber had been a girl I dated freshman year. It was a rough time to go through when all your buddies were dating and you were potty training your wife and teaching her how to tie her shoes. My parents were beginning to think of finding me a new mate, even Cat's parents were supportive. They said if I asked Cat for permission, they'd allow it. Of course the little girl had no idea, but she had let me date someone else. It was nothing like I imagined and, after only a couple weeks, I ended it. It was exciting the first couple dates until I realized I was cheating on my future wife, and I knew I'd rather have her.

To think Amber would come back in my life at my lowest point. I had let her in, needing someone to talk to. She told me she was moving in down the street for a new job closer downtown. Told me how she still wanted me and knew I wasn't bound yet. Amber was desperate and I could see that, but I didn't tell her to leave. Not even when her hand ran over my thigh and grazed my groin. It sent a zap right up my spine and it was so different than anything I ever felt. I thought it was enough, but I craved more of it. Her hands worked so well and, for once, I didn't have to worry about anyone else or doing anything but enjoying myself. I hadn't planned to let it go that far, or much longer after I got that first taste, but it blew my mind when she got me off. I didn't think anything could ruin my high, until I saw her face.

There was so much pain in Cat's eyes. More pain than I ever saw before, and that was coming from a lot. I saw skinned knees when she tried to roller skate. Bruises all over from learning to ice skate. Splinters, bumps, bruises, cuts and a broken finger from transformations and running through the woods. I saw her cry when we fought over candy bars and bed time, which stories and what pajamas. But nothing was like what I saw, and then from completely being shut out.

Our wedding was a week away and I knew it was too late for her parents to call it off. Too late because she was getting older and all the unclaimed guys wanted younger girls. Too late to find her a new mate. It was the only bit of relief I had, even if it meant that her parents could still end it and leave her single for her life. Maybe that would be better than a miserable life with me, but at least I could try to win her back.

I left her house hours later, still so unsure about our future. Her mom said they were going to push the wedding back a few weeks, that was if she got ahold of the elder in the morning. Cat didn't come see me or even listen in. I knew that because I didn't hear a little squeak of the step, third from the top. I couldn't lose her. Not when I loved her so much, and not like this.

# CHAPTER FOURTEEN

# *Cat*

"Mom, please," I begged. She told me that they, her and dad, had decided to move the wedding. That we just needed some time to sort things out. "There's nothing to sort out. He cheated on me! I don't want to see him again and I don't want to spend the rest of my life bound to him. Don't you want me to be happy?"

It was a low blow. I knew and they knew it. This whole new-thinking arrangement was supposed to be about a way to make my married life the happiest it could be by having love instead of learning to find it. It seemed like a worse idea that just the luck of the draw everyone else was getting. There were no deals and no lofty expectations there. Just paired up, bound, sex and litters. Feelings, love and emotions need not apply.

"Cat, I don't want you to regret it. You grew up with Leo. You love him." She just went about making lunch.

"But mom, he was with another girl!"

She stopped and looked up at me. "Cat, he didn't sleep with her. If we really want to get technical, you gave him permission to. This was the girl he asked you about years ago if he could date. Leo's still going to be bound to you and you're the one he wants. Not her."

Like that was any reassurance. "Just means he regrets me and still wants her. I saw her. She's prettier and his age and-"

"You stop thinking that. If that boy really wanted that girl, he would have left long ago."

"He never came to see me, mom. The day I told him about how I felt about litters and sex and all that was the day he went back to her." Not that I knew that for sure. Just why wouldn't he? He obviously had her number and must have called her.

My mom giggles and I want to yell at her for it, but she beats me to it. "Honey, he was here every night." And that knocks the wind out of my sails.

I just stared at her, confused, for the longest time. "What?" I squeaked. Not the best comeback, especially with the way I said it.

She just shrugged. "Yea, he came by every night. Talked to us for a couple hours and then would go upstairs and watch you sleep for a while. Said he couldn't stand not seeing you every day, so he'd do it this way." She paused to bring lunch over to the table. "Now that I think of it, I don't remember the last time you two weren't together all day."

I'm not sure what to say. I thought Leo had just given up and ignored me. I hadn't expected him to stop by. I knew he was hurt and probably upset, but he still wanted to see me. Now the tables were turned. It had been two days, and I knew he was the one that tossed pebbles at my window every night. I took a vicious bite out of my sandwich and brooded.

Not once had it crossed my mind to go see Leo or try to talk things out. Now I had my mom and her knowing smile to deal with. I was beginning to think she could be right. I might regret giving up on Leo, if there was a chance we could work things out. I sighed and set the rest of my sandwich on the plate.

"I'm going to Leo's." I sighed, getting up. I grabbed my phone to send him a quick text that I was coming over. Maybe this time, if he had a girl over, he'd get rid of her before I showed up and keep the illusion that he was perfect and things were fine going.

# CHAPTER FIFTEEN

It was a relief when he opened the door and I could see that he was alone. I had taken my time on the flight over, but hadn't come up with what I was going to say until I saw him. "I'm sorry."

I wasn't sure what expression read on his face, but his arms wrapped around me and pulled me close. "No, I'm sorry, sweetheart. I didn't mean for-"

"I love you," I cut him off. I didn't need to know why it happened. Leo loved me and some part of me already knew it was never going to happen again. But he needed to know that I still felt the same. That I still loved him.

For the second time in my life, I watched Leo cry. Only this time I was here and brushed them off his face. He buried his face in my shoulder, even though he was taller than me by a foot. I had never had to comfort him before and, while it should have felt awkward, it just felt right. Leo wasn't perfect. He was human, and he was my love.

"Leo, if you want... a litter, I... I'll do it." I'm pretty sure I said that, but my voice sounded so small.

"Cat, I don't want to force you into it. Sweetheart, I don't." He pulls back, just enough to look me in the eye. "I know you're scared and I know you'd be a great mother. And sweetheart, I'd be right next to you the whole time. I promise. I'll never leave you alone."

Leo pulled me back into his apartment and towards the couch before he thought better of it. He sat in the recliner and I curled up on his lap. My hand traced the lines of his palm as I weighted my words. "As long as it's with you," I started quietly, "I want to, Leo. You won't let things change. You... you won't let me change."

I rested my head on his shoulder this time and told him again how scared I was. I told him all my fears and he just listened until I had nothing else to say. Then we just held each other, listening to our heartbeats and the birds outside.

"Our wedding's in three days," he said softly. I nodded, letting him talk and listening to the timbre of his voice. "I know it's different for you. Parents don't tell their daughters what's going to happen until that day. Guys, we find out before we're even paired. It's great to hear what sex is like and then spend years fantasizing about it. I can't tell you how many times I imagined what we'd do."

His fingers are distracting me a little as it traces looping shapes on my shoulder, but he continues on. "At our wedding, after we say our vows to each other, we will be bound. There's two ways to do it, sweetheart, and they will ask me. The guy always chooses because everyone is ancient in thinking the man owns his bride, even if it's just for an hour. The elder will ask now or later. It's the ultimate fantasy to do it right then in front of all your family and friends and show them how good you are and what it looks to put a litter in someone. If I pick later, I have to bring our sheets to the elder and show him the blood from your first time."

I stiffened in his arms. I definitely didn't want to do it in front of everyone. I didn't want to have sex at all. "Leo, I-"

He places a finger over my lips to get me to stop. The look in his eyes reassures me and I don't try to fight him. Maybe that's been our problem. No one's ever fought their mate or been given as much freedom as I had.

"Cat, I've thought about it since you told me. If the elders found out, we'd both be in trouble but no one would imagine I'd lie. I'm a guy, after all." He shrugged. "We poke your finger and put a little blood on my sheets. I'll, do the rest."

I moved to kiss him, but there was a look on his face that told me there was more. "Sweetheart, just promise me... promise me that one day we'll do it. I don't care how long I have to wait for you, but promise that one day I'll get to make love to you."

There was my Leo, the one that never asked for anything. I kissed him softly. "I promise, Leo. One day we'll make love."

# CHAPTER SIXTEEN

# *Cat*

I feel sick to my stomach. I had picked the wrong dress and my hair is completely wrong. When I walked down that aisle and Leo saw me, he wasn't going to marry me. I paced in the back, waiting for the music to start. This was horrible!

"Cat, will you stop running in circles and sit? You're making me dizzy." Mae had decided to help me get ready. Really pregnant Mae, by the way. I was beginning to think it was because she wouldn't fit into the pews and this side room was the only one that had a folding chair. "Leo loves you. He's not going to care about anything but tearing that dress off you."

That's where Mae was mostly wrong. There wasn't going to be any dress tearing off or day-long sex like her wedding. I was going to walk down that aisle, say some words, and then that was it. "Mae, you don't understand," I groaned, plopping in the chair opposite her. I knew she didn't.

"Right." She patted her growing stomach. "No idea what a wedding and being bound is like." Mae rolled her eyes. "Stop overreacting, Cat."

The music started and she bound up out of that chair like there was an epic sale at the mall where you buy one tiny thing and get half the store. "That's your cue!"

My hands are shaking as I try to push back to keep her from throwing me to the wolves. She shoved me towards the doors in the back of the church and I froze. There were dozens of eyes fixed on me as I tried to regain my composure. The small bundle of flowers was almost falling out of my hands as I glanced up to see Leo standing there. With the biggest, warmest smile ever.

I was doing this for him. This was what he deserved. He deserved a day to be so complete and overwhelmingly happy, and I think it was starting to sink into me. Slowly, I started towards him, not really sure how I was moving without falling. His eyes never left me once and, when I reached him, I could tell he needed to kiss me. He took the flowers from my hand

and leaned in so close that I thought that was what he was doing.

As my eyes closed, I heard him whisper, "Sweetheart, you're gorgeous and I'm the luckiest guy in the world."

Leo leaned back and smiled down at me without so much as a touch. I knew we weren't supposed to until after the vows, but somehow not being able to feel him was turning me on. I wanted my Leo, and I knew he wanted me. My head was in such a fog as a stared at those gorgeous blue eyes and down at those soft lips that I wanted to feel whispering secrets against mine.

"Cat, do you?"

Suddenly, I know what a deer in the headlights thinks because that's me as the elder repeats the questions. I can hear someone snickering in the back of the hall, so I know this isn't the first time it has been posed to me. I glance at Leo, terrified that I'm ruining this day for him but there's nothing but a smile as he ever so slightly nods.

"I do... promise to love and cherish you; to be your faithful wife and bear your litters." I stumble a little near the end. It's not so much the nerves at this point, but how his thumbs gently caress the back of my hands as he holds them. I have no idea if it's more to help me get through this ceremony or to ease my mind that I was already breaking the vows.

Leo didn't falter once as he repeated the words to me. Pledging a love that I already knew and devoting a life to me. I had almost lost him once and we both knew that was a mistake we wouldn't soon forget. His eyes never showed a glimmer of disappointment when he promised to lay with me and grow a family.

"Do you wish to consummate this union now or later?" The elder directed the question to Leo, but I knew it was really my call. It wasn't supposed to the woman's choice. The woman wasn't supposed to have a clue what would happen until moments before she walked down the aisle to her husband. But Leo knew how loaded this question was. I couldn't help but picture two versions of what must be playing out in his head – showing off his love by taking me on the mattress or keeping me all to himself, savoring his time learning my body. There was always a chance that he'd be selfish, for once. It seemed like everyone was holding their breath for his answer.

"Later," he said softly. And that smile was just for me before his lips finally kissed mine.

# CHAPTER SEVENTEEN

# Cat

I can't believe it. We're married! When Leo kissed me, people actually started to cheer like they do in the movies. And my *husband* had on the sexiest smile ever. It was all just perfect. He squeezed my hand gently as he led me up the aisle. More like run, but I could tell he was just as excited as I was. He took me into the side room near the entrance and closed the door.

"Finally! You're all mine." His grin was huge as he leaned in to kiss me. His hands pulled me close and I could feel something pressing back into my stomach. Leo rubbed his hips against me, and I'm pretty sure it wasn't something we talked about.

"Leo?" I manage to pull back but with the door behind my back there's nowhere I can go. I shouldn't be afraid of my husband, but I'm starting to feel it. I can see a bed laying out over his shoulder. "Why is there a bed? Leo, I thought you said we'd go home and have cake."

He chuckles. "Because it's for us. I said later, sweetheart. There's no way I can share what's mine, even a look, and you can't expect me to wait forever. I waited this long!"

"But Leo, you said after I was done with school and you wouldn't pressure me."

Leo reaches out for me and I can't do anything to get away from his grasp. He reaches for my left arm, but I move right and around him. I'm in an even worse position, as the bed's behind me now. When he starts laughing, it sends chills up my spine.

"Who do you think you are, sweetheart? You're my *wife.* You're my *property* now. You do what I say, and I say we're getting on that bed and fucking. All day, even if you pass out." He stalks towards me. "There's not going to be any school for you. You're going to have my litters, one after another."

I'm shaking now. He had lied to me the whole time. That hurts more than anything he's going to do to me now, on that bed. "Leo, if you do this, I'll hate you forever." My voice is just as shaky as the rest of me.

He just laughs. "Like I care what you think. Get on the bed." When I don't move, he starts yelling. "Get on the bed!"

Leo shoves me backward and I'm falling. I'm going to land on the bed and he's going to tear apart my wedding dress and rape me. I can see it in his eyes. I'm screaming, and it feels like forever until I hit the bed.

I jolt up in bed, trying to catch my breath. It felt like someone is trying to suffocate me. Leo stirs a little, but remains asleep. It takes a while to realize where I am and that it was just a dream. Slipping out of bed and the tangle of Leo's limbs, I step into my slippers and head down to the kitchen to get a glass of water.

The dream felt so real and my hands are still shaking as I take a glass out of the cupboard and fill it with cool water. The water does little to shake the nightmare. I move to sit at the table, not trusting myself to remain standing and composed. What's got me the most is how feel that Leo felt and knowing badly he wants more.

"Sweetheart?" I jump at the sound of his sleepy voice behind me. He walks up and wraps his arms around my shoulders over the back of the chair. "What are you doing awake?"

He yawns while I debate how to answer that. There's the version where it was just a matter of being thirsty. Then there was the truth, a nightmare about what our wedding could have been and who he might be. Leo will definitely spot the lie but maybe he won't question it, seeing as he wasn't quite awake. The latter would only crush him, and I couldn't hurt him again.

"Just a bad dream. I thought I'd get a drink before coming back to bed." It was half-truths. A way out of lying unless Leo asked for more. A way not to hurt him.

He moves the glass out of my hands and pulls me up into his arms. "Come to bed?"

A simple nod is all it takes to get that goofy grin on his face and a kiss. That smile could get anything in the world, and he's used it for such evils. I rest my head on his shoulder as we walk back. It's odd to see all my things here and there with his. Part of me can't accept that I don't have a home to go to because it's here now, and always going to be Leo's. The greater part loved how our two worlds melted together. Then again, he's been expecting this for eighteen years. It's like Leo had purposely left spots for me to fill in.

He slips under the sheets behind me and holds me close, wrapping my body in his. "Want to tell me about it?" Leo asks softly.

It wasn't that he was letting me off the hook, but letting me get out the demons in his protective arms. I take a deep breath, knowing I can't play off being asleep and I couldn't run to the bathroom, or anywhere else for that matter. It took some effort and time, but it all got out and we both seemed to have survived it.

Leo was quiet for a long time after I finished and I started to think he had fallen asleep. "Cat, you know I'd never do that, right?" His voice was soft as he tried to reassure me of that. I knew he wouldn't force himself on me, but my future was still a little hazy now. I would be graduating next week and we hadn't planned anything pass the wedding, except that we'd play it by ear when the sex would actually happen. I had promised him that we'd get to experience it once and I wanted him, but there was such a fear in that.

"I will never hurt you like that. You promised me that we'll make love one day, and that was and is good enough for me. I know when it goes happen that it'll be just that much more special." He kisses the back of my shoulder gently. "I know we haven't talked much about things after the wedding. Is that something you want to do, sweetheart? Do you want to go to college?"

His voice is just as gentle as his affectionate reassurance, but I know what's underneath it. Leo would never admit it, but college was going to be a stretch. His job had done fine to keep him afloat, but now he had to support me, instead of my parents. Besides having another mouth to feed, now he'd have to save up for tuition in addition to probably paying off some student loans he had left. It didn't seem fair, yet at the same time I knew he'd do it for me. "I'd like to, but I'm not really sure for what. I've always liked writing, so maybe journalism." It wasn't as great as whatever he did at the bank, but at least there was the city newspaper or magazines I could try to write for.

"Sounds perfect for you, and you can probably even work from home. No missed meals. No empty bed to come home to." *And nothing to keep us from having a litter or two?* I want to ask him if that's part he's left unsaid. I've seen the way he's looked at his friends' kids. Hell, even the random babies we pass on the walk to the grocery store. And there's no doubt he'd be a great father. If only he had picked someone else, but I know I'd never be as happy with anyone else.

"I can get a job too," I added quietly.

"Whatever you want, sweetheart." It's barely a whisper, but it somehow ends the discussion. Maybe it's due to the fact it's now four in the morning and he'll have to get up in a couple hours to make breakfast before he leaves. No missed meals, none.

CHAPTER EIGHTEEN

# Cat

"Spill."

I roll my eyes as I sit across from Mae at the lunch tables. It's one of the last days like this that we'll have. She looks ready to pop right now and I desperately hope I won't have to witness that. From what I've heard from the gossip in the girls' bathroom, it's bloody and messy and just gross. But at least it's her and not me...

"Come on, I told you all the juicy bits with Derek." As if I wanted to know what she was doing with her husband. The guy was half a foot shorter than her with freckles and the oddest shade of red hair ever. He was definitely not someone Mae would have picked out for herself, but there were parts she was obsessed with.

Like his butt dimples, fuzzy chest hair, and his penis. Yes, his penis. I'd gotten to know *him* as well as one could without actually meeting it.

"And why should I have to tell you about Leo?" I knew as soon as I said it that I would regret it. I hadn't thought her obsession with him would last past both our bindings, but it had. It almost looked like Mae was hurt I wouldn't tell her. Maybe this was what claimed women did, chatting about their husbands and pregnancy cravings. If only Mae knew...

"Because I'm your best friend? Because you got the hottest guy, like, ever?" She takes a sip of her diet cola. "Because we promised each other as kids that we'd tell each other everything, especially how good he is in bed."

"We never promised that!"

Mae rolls her eyes. "Okay, maybe not the last but we did promise to tell each other everything. And I already told you everything about Derek. Okay, well, not everything. I didn't tell you about how he sneezes when he comes."

I try to block out that imagine, but it just adds to everything else in my head about the guy. My body shivers on its own and I try to resist the urge to toss my cookies. Especially when it actually is a cookie, and one of the last ones my mom sent over after the wedding. Raspberry white chocolate chip, yum!

"But I never asked you." I try to build my defense. It's weak, and we both know it. But how am I supposed to know all that about Leo? Even though there's no way that she'd know, it feels like somehow Mae would catch the lie. Leo always does and Mae's known me for almost as long.

"You should want to tell me. Remember that time you got that red flyer girl toy? You couldn't stop tell me about how you put it on the launcher and how high she twirls up when you pull the string, and how pretty her fairy outfit was. You went on for days about a silly toy, but you haven't said a word about your yummy hubby?" She leaned forward and she squinted, like she could see the answers written all over my face. Mentally, I tried to hide all the secrets with Leo, just in case she did have some sort of super-power. "So, either he's completely horrible or he's a sex god and you don't want me to steal him."

I did not see that coming. "Um, well..." I start but she cuts me off.

"That proves it!" She points at me, almost tipping over my milk carton. "He's hung like a horse and knows how to rock it!" People are starting to look now. "I knew there was no way he could be that hunky and have a tiny dick. So how big is he?"

Her face gets closer to my reddening one. "I don't know... big?" I'm not going to be able to do this.

There's no way that I can convince her I've slept with, much less seen, Leo.

"What like six or seven inches long?"

I know I should just ignore her and change the subject. I shouldn't be fueling the fire, but Mae's right. We tell each other everything, even if now it had to be my lies.

"Six and a half." I wanted to go with the larger one, but what if she could tell Leo wasn't? The middle seemed the safest.

She smiles and nods. "Got new respect for you, Cat. Didn't think you'd be able to handle that, tiny." Mae teases. All because I was a late bloomer, in just about everything including my height.

"I'm surprised he lets you come to school. If I was him, I wouldn't."

"What are you talking about, Mae?"

She sighs heavily like it's so obvious. "Well, you said he gets up early to make breakfast for you before he goes to work. And Leo cleans and all that stuff." It's strange how it takes someone else to point out things before they sink in. "It's just those are sorta wife things. But you must be on him the rest of the time he's home. I mean, that's a fair trade for guys. The whole reason they want to get bound to someone is for the sex. That whole need to procreate thing is basically ancient history." She rolls her eyes and finishes her drink.

"Mae, hypothetically, what if I wasn't sleeping with him?"

She stares at me for a moment, trying to figure out where such a question could come from. Maybe she thinks we're fighting or maybe she'll realize we haven't done it. Mae grabs her empty soda can and gets up.

"Then you'd be horrible," she says flatly.

I watch her walk away and I can't help but feel horrible. Guilt over all Leo does for nothing in return. Guilt over not pulling his clothes off and getting between the sheets. Guilt over being a disappointment to                                                     him.

# CHAPTER NINETEEN

I walk into the living room. Leo's made dinner again, and not just something quick from frozen or take-out. He actually made lasagna from scratch and didn't even burn the garlic bread. He's on the couch reading the newspaper. As I snuggle into his side, I realize I don't understand him at all. Not only was there dinner, but he helped me study for my last final and now he was going to let me invade his time. Yet he never asks for anything.

"Leo, can I ask you something?" I ask quietly as I rest my head on his shoulder. It looks like this weekend's forecast is sunny and in the 60s.

"Mhmm."

He's not exactly paying attention. Clearly the scores of last night's game is more interesting than me, but I understand it's just his "me time". Although, I had a feeling that wouldn't be the case much longer.

"I want to try something." I want for him to say something or put down the newspaper, but he's not biting. Maybe it was just a sign that this should wait. It's just that I couldn't keep facing Mae and avoiding this forever. It wasn't what I promised, but I had to try to get there. "Want a blowjob?"

"What?!" Leo coughed, trying to cover up his surprise.

That seemed to get his attention. I rested a hand on his knee and slowly started up his leg. "A blowjob. You know. I undo your pants and put my mouth arou-"

"I know what it is," he cut me off and stopped my hand. "I just... um, where's this coming from, sweetheart?"

He's set aside the newspaper. I have his full attention now. It seems there's a little more attention coming, and I have to stop staring at his crotch. I had thought Leo would have jumped at this. After all, he let that other girl put her hand down his pants. Maybe I was wrong.

"I just thought we could try it," I say quietly. My hands fidget with the hem of my shirt. "Because we haven't done it." I'm starting to regret saying anything.

"You know, nevermind. I'll just let you get back to the paper and..."

I start to get up, but he gently pulls me back down beside him. He won't let go of my hand and his thumb runs softly back and forth.

"I didn't say no, sweetheart." He smiles softly. "I just wanted to know why all of a sudden you wanted to do something."

Because you're perfect and sexy, and I'm an idiot for making you wait. Because I might want to have sex soon and want to ease into it. Because I don't want you finding some other girl to do things to you. Because I love you. Because I want to.

None of them really felt good enough reasons. Leo would have accepted any of them, except maybe the fondling by other girls part.

There's a hundred things that I could say, but none that I want to say. The silence between us is starting to feel awkward, and he's looking at me expectantly. I started this, so I know I'm the one that needs to start talking.

"Have you ever had one before?" I ask quietly, blushing at the thought of something dirty. It was amazing that I got this far with-out looking so naïve.

"A blowjob?" He raises an eyebrow. Clearly this wasn't the exact path we thought this would take. "No, I never got one. Sweetheart, my heart and body were yours since the day I saw you. Other than the one slip up with my ex, no one has done anything to me, except my hand." His smile's half-hearted from his admission, and I can't stop my face from turning crimson.

"I'd love to get a blowjob from you, sweetheart."

I know he's trying to be supportive. It's in his voice. And why wouldn't he? Leo gets all the benefit from it. Well maybe not all. I'd finally get to see that half of him naked. It's only fair after the countless bath times he helped catch me for. My parents sure loved having someone do their dirty work for them.

Biting my bottom lip, my hands reach down and graze his pants. It's just a button and a zipper, but it might as well be Fort Knox. My fingers are shaking a little after popping the button and slowly tugging the zipper down. I know what I'm going to find, but at the same time I don't. I was finally going to see the rest of Leo, and it was an odd kind of thrill. Mae's questions started to bubble up again. Was he big? Have a "treasure trail"? Freckles on his balls?

He's warm and solid when I finally reach my hand in through the flap of his underwear. I'm not sure what I had expected. Maybe something spongier? Mae made it sound like getting it hard was a big change, and he didn't feel like a flabby goo-filled sack of skin. Maybe he was already hard?

"Are you okay?" Leo asked softly.

He has to be thinking that I'm regretting this, but I'm not. "Isn't it supposed to be more... squishy?"

I pull my hand back when I feel him twitch under my palm while he laughs. It's such an odd feeling. It feels like it's alive. Like it's something with a mind of its own, not really part of Leo.

"No, sweetheart. It's not really... squishy." He tries not to laugh. "It is softer now." Leo smiles softly as he leans over and kisses me. "But you'll change that. I don't want you to freak out, sweetheart. It is going to... perk up."

I nod slowly and look back at the appendage peeking out the top of his clothing. It wasn't that scary looking. Slowly, I slide my hand into his bottoms and wrap my hand around him. I can see him tense up and it twitches again. I take him out of his underwear and really get a look at it. It reminds me of a cross between a mushroom and big finger, if they had holes at the ends. I move my thumb back and forth over the tip, feeling the dip at the opening. Leo groans a little and I start to panic.

"I'm sorry." I stop. "Am I hurting you?" Maybe it was the wrong thing to do with it.

He shakes his head. "God, no. It feels good, sweetheart." Leo leans his head back. "I can't stop thinking what it's going to feel like to be in your mouth."

"My mouth?" Oh, yea... blowjob. I had kind of forgotten about that when I finally saw him. He starts to say something, probably about how it would be fine if I didn't, but I kiss him instead of letting his words get out. I want to do this.

I moved off the couch and knelt in front of him. Glancing up, I could see his eyes following me and wondering what I would do next. The steps weren't hard to follow. Put in mouth, bob head up and down, done. He was twitching more in my hand and Leo was right about perking up. It probably would stand right up even without being held. I lean close enough that I could just slip it in my mouth. I want to be great for Leo, to make him forget what that other girl did it him.

Leo gasps when I let him slip pass my lips. His skin is just a little salty and his smell is so... manly sexy Leo. It's like a new flavor and I want to taste more. I follow down the underside of him with my tongue. His body shivers and I hear him moan.

I want to make my Leo feel like he never has before. I want to make love to him the only way I can right now. I want him to know how much I truly love him.

# CHAPTER TWENTY

I feel dizzy. There's something wrong with me, and I'm not completely sure that I believe it. I had hoped for so long that I was just under the weather and that was the reason my transformations were taking so long. Sure they lasted only a few seconds longer, but I wasn't used to seeing the process. This morning when I turned into a sparrow to fly home, I saw my body completely turn the shade of blackened grey before shrinking and feeling the feathers slip out from under my skin. Turning back was the same, when I turned into a small flesh tone figure before the glow turned me back human.

It was something I had sort of expected to hear from my mother, but hearing it made it all so much more real. I gently run my hand over my slightly plump stomach while she gets me a cup of honey tea. I'd hidden it fairly easily from Leo, seeing as it was Fall now. Sweaters and the elastic-banded leggings were my friends.

"You should tell him, Cat." She sets the cup in from of me before sitting across the table with her own. "Leo's going to be so happy."

I can tell that she is too, but trying to hold it back. I've finally told her how terrified I am about giving birth, and there's no way to avoid that now that I'm pregnant. "I don't know how, mom."

She laughs. "Sweetie, it's easy. Just say, 'honey, I'm pregnant'. Or you could let him see your stomach. Actually see it without that bulky sweater."

"Mom, maybe I'm just getting fat. Leo's a great cook. I don't want him to get his hopes up. We only did it once, on his birthday," I quietly admit before sipping the steaming cup of tea. How could one time really get me pregnant?

"Sweetie, sometimes all it takes is once."

I pace the kitchen while the chicken bakes in the oven. Leo will be home from work soon and I've decided to tell him. I also figured I should make dinner. If nothing else, being the one to cook would distract him from what I'm wearing and buy me a little more time to work up my courage. I had thought wearing one of my favorite dresses would give me that, but it was a little tight now and showed the bump.

The timer goes off and I slip the oven mitts on to get out the two pans in the oven. Mom had told me how to make a simple, delicious dinner. I make up two plates and set them on the candlelit table. I really had tried to go all out for him.

"Sweetheart, I'm home!"

I hear him come in and the butterflies flutter again in my stomach. How could there be room for butterflies anymore with a baby inside me? I run my hand back and forth over my stomach as I wait for Leo to come in the dining room. His footsteps are getting closer and I chicken out, sitting so he can't see the baby bump.

"Wow. What's all this?" There a big smile on his face as he walks around the table to kiss me. "Chicken Parmesan and roasted red potatoes. Yum."

I watch as he goes to get something to drink and sits across from me. "I just wanted to do something nice, and I know I should be doing more. I mean, you go to work and do all the work. All I do is going to a class or two."

He sighs and looks up at me. "Sweetheart, I told you that I don't care about that. I can cook."

"But I want to take care of you now. You took care of me my whole life and... I don't know how much longer I'll be able to."

His fork drops and hits the plate. "What do you mean, sweetheart? Are you... are you sick?"

Leo's face went pale. The worst had to be going through his head and I couldn't let him suffer with those thoughts. I took a deep breath and moved to stand but my legs feel like jelly, so I remain sitting.

"Leo, I'm pregnant."

His face twitches a little as it fights for which emotion to show first. All I see before he's attacking me with kiss after kiss, is a huge smile stealing his face.

# CHAPTER TWENTY ONE

Leo decided to take the day off of work to come with me. I told him that he didn't have to, that I could get my mom to come with me, but he wouldn't listen to reason. He had to work so that we could have things for the baby.

"Sweetheart, this is our baby. I'm going to be here for everything." His hands rest on either side of my stomach as I sit on the examining room table. "I promised I'd be by your side."

The technician comes in as he places a soft kiss on my lips. I don't think I could love this man any more than I already do. And I'm really hoping it's a litter. It's the only thing I can do for all his love.

"Okay, Cat, just lay back on the table and we'll see how the little one is doing."

I lay back and let the woman lift my shirt and pull down my leggings. She squirts a bit of the gel on my abdomen and I jump because it's colder than I would have expected. Leo's holding my hand, but his eyes are glued to the small screen as the woman moves the wand over me. I know that screen is going to show us the baby, or babies, inside me but I can't stop watching his face. I see his eyes get big and his mouth hangs open. I have to see what's got him looking like that.

I turn my head to see the screen and watch as two little peanuts moving in and out of focus. *Two babies!* It's not quite a litter but we're going to be parents.

"Looks like only two want to come see mommy and daddy."

"Only two?" I stare at the woman and see her smile.

She nods. "There's a shadow of one in the back there." The technician points to a spot on the screen. "The monitor is picking up four heartbeats, besides mommy's."

Leo squeezes my hand and it's all that's keeping me from drifting off in my own thoughts and fears. I have no idea how I'm going to give birth to four babies, let alone raise them all. I know I won't be able to do it on my own and I'm not sure we'll be able to afford all of them, but giving up a baby isn't a possibility. I couldn't give up part of Leo. I wouldn't be able to live with myself.

The woman prints off a photo and hands it to Leo before wiping off the gel on me. She congratulates us again before leaving us alone for a while. I fix my clothes and sit up. Leo is standing next to me and I lean over to see our babies.

"Are you happy?" I ask, looking up from the photo in his hands.

He chuckles. "Of course I am, sweetheart. Look at this." He points to the photo. "We're going to have a litter, four wonderful little babies."

Leo kisses my cheek. "Are you happy, sweetheart? I know this probably isn't what you wanted."

I smack his arm. "I'm having your babies. Why wouldn't I be happy?" Although I already know what he'll say. "I'll get through it, Leo. I just can't think about what's going to happen and think about all the things we'll do as a family."

I get off the table and kiss him. "Let's go home. I want to put that on the fridge." I can't stop smiling.

# CHAPTER TWENTY TWO

# *Leo*

"Sweetheart, please." I hate begging, but something like this she should be hopping in the car for.

She just shook her head and started down at her stomach. If I hadn't heard it straight from the doctor's mouth, I wouldn't have been able to tell she was three months along. Three long, stubborn months. Three long months of reading baby books and appointments.

I groan as I sit down next to her on the couch. "Cat, I can tell there's something wrong and I know you do too." I take her hands and hold them in mine. "You haven't been transforming at all lately. You whimper in pain while you sleep. Sweetheart... I've been smelling blood."

The worst part is not knowing if it's her or the babies. I love all of them; but, while I'd be torn up about losing our kids, I would be beyond devastated if I lost her. This fear had been bubbling up with every little problem since we found out Cat was having a litter.

"Please, let me take you to the hospital." I was getting to the point where I was just going to throw her over my shoulder and drag her there.

"Leo, you're overreacting. I just like walking more and getting some exercise that way. And I'm sure I'm not "whimpering in pain". I'm probably groaning because I have a litter inside me playing rock star on my insides."

She slowly gets up and waddles a little ways before stopping and glancing over her shoulder. "Coming to bed?"

CHAPTER TWENTY THREE

"Leo!"

I can't move. I'm not sure what's happening. The only thing I can hope is that he hasn't left the apartment yet. The pain is getting unbearable and my vision is blurring from the tears.

"Leo, help!" I croak out.

I hear footsteps running back to the room. I need him, and I need him bad.

"Sweetheart, what's... oh my god."

That's not what I want to hear. I need him to tell me how it'll be okay. There's only two months left before my due date and I haven't gotten far enough in the baby book to know if this is normal or not.

Leo looks paler than a ghost and I know something's wrong. His hands shakes as he pulls out his cell phone. He dials as he slowly creeps closer.

"I need an ambulance. It's my wife... she's in bed and can't move and... and there's a lot of blood."

Blood? I try to reach down with my hand through the pain. My fingers disappear behind my stomach and there's something sticky. My fingers are red and drenched in blood. *Oh my god...*

I pass out just as I hear the sirens.

Leo won't go back to work. He's taken time off and he's made himself my slave. I've given up arguing with him. I have no fight left anymore.

"Sweetheart, it's time for your pills," he said softly.

He sits down on the couch next to me with a glass of water and pill bottle. I haven't moved from my perch in days, but it's nothing new. I didn't move once in the three days they kept me at the hospital after the miscarriage. But I've just felt like an empty shell, like I'm not even here. I know Leo's worried, and that's why he's stayed. He has to force me to take my pills and even to eat. I just don't know how he can still be with me after I lost our babies.

The tears start again. I can't stop thinking about all the blood and the smell. All I can smell is death and no matter how many times he bathes me, it doesn't change. Leo sets the glass and pills down on the coffee table and pulls me into his arms.

"It's okay, sweetheart." He rubs my back, but I'm crumbling more.

"No, it's not." My voice feels rough in my throat. "I killed our babies." I can't stop crying. Leo's told me a hundred times that it isn't my fault, but I know it is. I had to have done something wrong, otherwise our babies would still be here.

# CHAPTER TWENTY FOUR

# Leo

I watch her and I know something's up. I haven't seen Cat like this in months. She keeps staring out the window. I walk up behind her and wrap my arms around her. Did she just flinch?

"Sweetheart, are you okay?" I kiss her cheek and rest my head on her shoulder.

She's quiet for way too long. Did she lose her job? Did she fail that exam?

"I think I'm pregnant again, Leo."

Cat just keeps staring out the window. Now I know what's going through her mind. She's thinking about the miscarriage. Probably worrying that we'll lose this baby. I hope she doesn't slip away from me again. I have no idea how to help her when she seems so lost and dead to the world. I was finally getting her back to the Cat I loved.

"That's great, sweetheart."

"Leo, what if..."

I don't let her say it. "We'll have a healthy baby. And we can even finish the nursery. All we need to do is put together the crib and get some baby clothes." I kiss her cheek again. "Think about all those cute little socks."

I feel her lean back against me. She's crying. If there was any way to guarantee things would be alright, I'd do anything and I tell her so. Cat brushes the tears from her eyes and manages a small smile.

"I know," she says quietly.

Cat closes her eyes and I can feel her moving her hand back and forth across her belly. I think she'll come back around and be excited again to be pregnant. I just wish I didn't have to hide how overjoyed I was. It was going to take all my will power not to call our parents tonight and tell them.

"I love you, Leo." She tilts her head up and kisses my cheek. I can't help but give her a little squeeze in reply.

"I love you too, sweetheart.

"What did you do?"

I shake my head and stare at my wife. Her face is turning beet red, so she must have tried to get away with something. I hand her a cup of hot chocolate and watch her carefully take a sip. I'm just waiting now for her to add the whipped cream to her nose and complete the outfit.

"I'm gone for ten minutes and you managed to get covered in paint." I reach out to wipe a splotch of it from her cheek. "I thought we agreed that I'd be the lucky one to huff the fumes and you got to set up the dresser."

"But I already folded the clothes and got them tucked away. And the diapers are already stacked in the closet." Cat sighs. "I just thought I'd help and maybe we could go out and do something. You know, one last day out before the babies come."

She's smiling and I know she's imagining our three little ones. There was still one more crib to put together. We had decided to hold off until she was close to her due date, but that was only a week away now.

"Depends on what you have in mind, sweetheart."

The blush creeps back onto her cheeks and I can't help but get caught up in my adorable wife for a moment. We were all happy and all healthy, for once. My sweet little Cat was back to her old self and my love for her more than double.

"I was thinking of going to the movies and seeing the new RomCom, then maybe getting cheesecake at the café."

I'm not sure what I expected her to say, but a night out with her sounds great. "Well, you'll have to let me clean up the mess. And if you're going to go out, you probably should change and wash that paint off your face."

I laugh as she sticks her tongue out at me and heads to our bedroom down the hall. I put the lids back on the cans of paint and rinse the brushes off in the guest bathroom. By the time I make it to the bedroom to change out of my grungy clothes, Cat's almost dressed. Luckily, with her pregnant body, it won't take me long to catch up and beat her out the door.

"Should I get a taxi or do you want to fly? I know you're changing for four now." I can't help smiling. There's no way we're losing these babies and we're so close to the due date. I can't wait to be a father. It's been a long time coming.

"I can still fly, Leo." She rolls her eyes and goes to grab her purse. I know it's mostly filled with prenatal vitamins and health bars. It's almost like she's overdoing it for this pregnancy, but I have a feeling it's the only thing keeping her sane. It's the only way that she feels in control.

I probably shouldn't let her. What if her wings get tired and she drops out of the sky? Or what if a hawk snatches her up? I know that I'm being slightly irrational.

"I just don't want you to push yourself because of me." Or rather because she thinks we can't afford one measly taxi fare. "If you get tired, promise me you'll land and let me carry you."

Cat sighs. "I promise I will land and let you carry."

I give her a kiss. Her humoring me is what keeps me sane. I take her hand and hold it in mine as we walk out of our apartment and I lock up. I reluctantly let go of her hand and wait for her to transform. It's so strange to see it as if it's happening in slow-motion. It only takes me a split second to turn into a robin. I tilt my head and look at my sparrow wife before taking to the air. Hopefully the mile flight won't be too much for her.

I try to keep her in my line of sight, but her little wings had a hard time keeping up to mine. I slowed down as much as I could without falling from the sky myself. But we managed to make it. Cat took her time to change back. She was clearly tired and I was more determined to get us a taxi to the café down the street from home.

"Are you alright, sweetheart?"

I wrap my arm around her waist once she's transformed. She doesn't make a move to head in the theater. It's starting to worry me that she's closed her eyes and hasn't opened them. It's literally been minutes and I'm starting to worry she's passed out or something. I know she'd tell me to take a chill pill, there's probably something in that purse to do the trick.

"Just a little tired. I should have picked a robin too." She sighs.

I know it's not really that, but I'm not going to pick a fight to ruin our night.

"But you're my cute little sparrow." I kiss her cheek. With her mercurial pregnancy mood swings, I hope she doesn't take the flight choice to heart.

"I think I'm ready to go in." She smiles up at me. "Don't want to miss the movie."

"No, we don't."

I smile as we walk in together. Holding her hand, I love how I can show off that she's mine and that she's bearing my children. It's a bit of that mentality my parents hoped I wouldn't develop, but I feel like it's different. It's less of the proud Neanderthal "look what I've got, I'm awesome" and more of pride and love of how lucky and blessed I've been.

She doesn't say anything as I help her find a seat in the theater first. I know Cat's going to want popcorn with extra butter and a box of Junior Mints. It's just with these pregnancy cravings, I don't know what I know.

"What would you like me to get you?"

Cat smiles sweetly up at me. "Licorice and something not fizzy to drink, like juice if they have it."

Score eighty-nine for pregnancy cravings, zero for me. I'm going to end up getting the popcorn and candy too. I'm smart enough to know she'll want it either when the movie starts or we're on our way home or just about to go to bed. Besides, I love the overpriced theater popcorn. For as sarcastic as that sounds, there's just something better tasting about it than the microwave kind.

"I'll be right back." I kiss her cheek before heading out to the concessions.

There's a little bit of a line and I hope I don't end up missing the movie. I really don't want to wait in line just to walk in to help her out of the seat. By the time I get our snacks, the previews are just wrapping up. It's a bit darker than I'd like and it takes me a couple of minutes to spot where I left my wife. I shuffle pass a few other movie goers and take my rightful spot.

Handing her the licorice, Cat reaches for the box of candy. Oh, what a fickle beast these cravings are. I laugh a little to myself as I set her bottle of water in the cup holder. Who ever heard of juice at a movie theater? And I'd lie rather than tell her I could have gotten something less healthy for her and our babies. I know it was a bit irrational, but I didn't pick up the baby books after the miscarriage. For all I knew soda would cause a birth defect where they'd have three arms or eight eyes or a unicorn horn. That wasn't a risk I was willing to take and something I couldn't put Cat through. Water was good and she needed to stay hydrated. It was very reluctantly that I got one too. It wouldn't be fair to have that delicious sugar rush only to feel her glaring at me as I sucked up the soda through the striped straw.

I'm not sure what this movie's even supposed to be about. Cat seems happy and into it, at least for the first half hour. Then she's snoozing with her head on my shoulder. There's nothing I can do but sigh. She's been so exhausted with this pregnancy and a dark room lit only by a two people kissing on the screen. It wasn't a horrible movie, but it felt like I watched this one alone and it definitely wasn't something I'd pick. When it's done, I take the box of half eaten candy from her hand and gently shake her shoulder.

"Sweetheart, the movie's done." She stirs a little, but only to try and snuggle closer. "It's time to go home. Get that cheesecake." She mumbles a little at the sound of dessert, but it's barely enough to roust her.

"Cat, I'll eat it all myself." She mumbles something about me being a jerk. "We can finally pick out baby names?" It's the last bribe I have. I've tried to put it off, thinking it might jinx things. I had told her a couple names for the last ones, and they all died way too soon.

She sits up slowly. "Really?" A smile hints at her face and it grows when I nod.

I help her get moving. The air's crisp when we walk out of the movie theater and the sun's hanging low. It just feels so good and the smile on her face tells me that Cat wouldn't be opposed to walking now. I had every intention of getting cheesecake, but we end up at home before I knew it. The whole walk back had been about baby names and Cat's desperate attempts to make me agree on one of them.

"Leo, we have three babies. Why can't you pick even one name?" She sighed as she crawled into bed beside me. Her pajama tank top slipped up a little and she tugged it down over her belly again.

"Because none of them feel right. I can't picture myself at the park pleading with a Brock or Cameron to come down the slide so that we can go home for dinner. I'm sorry, Cat, but I'm not naming one of our babies Juniper either."

She sighs and rests her head on my chest. There are cogs working to think up more names. I know *somewhere* in this place is the baby name book. It had disappeared with the other half dozen books after the miscarriage.

"How about Michael?"

I open my mouth to tell her the name wouldn't stick, but I don't say anything. That name's not bad. Michael.

Mike. Mikey. Yea, he could do Michael. I smile. "That's one boy down, two to go."

"What?" She shifts and turns so her chin is on my chest and she's glaring at me. "There's no way I'm having three boys."

It's hard to stifle my laugh with her being so serious. "And why not? You don't think I'm stud enough to put three rowdy boys inside you?" It's a tad sexist, but this is my ego at stake!

Cat playfully punches my arm. "You know you're a stud after sticking me with two litters." She sighs. "It's just... I feel like there's a girl." Her eyes meet mine and I see mischief sparking. "I bet they're all girls."

Oh my sassy little wife! I tickle her and got her squirming. Only when she threatened to wet the bed did I stop. There was no way I was sleeping on soiled sheets. When babies started to invade their bed then I might learn to deal.

When she caught her breath, Cat laid in the crook of my arm, resting on her side with a hand tenderly rubbing over her bump. "I wanna call our girl Amber."

"No." I had to shut that down fast. There was no way I wanted to give my little girl the same name as the ex-girlfriend I cheat on Cat with. I knew that she didn't know my ex's name and I hated seeing the hurt on her face, but I knew if she learned why that it would be unbearable.

"What about Rae then?"

I rolled my eyes. "Did Mae suggest that?" I'd bet that she did. She probably wanted her best friend's kid's name to rhyme with hers. "Besides, it sounds like Ray and I don't want our baby girl being thought of as a boy."

I could tell that she wasn't enjoying this as much as she thought, and I know it's mostly my fault. Okay, so it was all my fault. I hadn't even suggested one name. "How about Ember? It's close to Amber but it," I had to think quick of a way to spin it off. "It's like a fire starting. Kind of like how things started for us. Your love for me started as an ember and eventually because a fire like mine was for you. We can give her Rae as a middle name."

"Ember Rae... makes me think love and sunny." She smiled and leaned up to kiss me. "I love your name."

It wasn't really my idea, but I had to stop being so negative against picking out names. "If you're sure there's at least one little girl in there, let's pick two boy and two girl names." Cat nodded. "We have two. That just means we need to agree on two more."

As if that hadn't been hard enough. Now it seemed we were set on two different versions of our babies. I knew we were having all boys, but I still had to humor her with that crazy girl idea. The silence was starting to get awkward with us both quietly thinking up a name to trump the other up and claim our versions were better. If anything, Cat would play dirty and stop after we decided on another girl's name and leave me hanging. I was too afraid to jinx this to bring it up again.

"Sam."

We paused, staring at each other. Did we both just say the same name, at the same time? Cat started giggling, and I knew we must have.

"Did we just pick all our babies names?" I stare at her, unable to believe that it wasn't really that difficult.

"I guess so, seeing as Sam could be both."

Cat runs her hand over her bump again, looking thoughtful. "Michael, Sam and Ember." The smile on her face is hard to miss. "You have one stubborn daddy, but I love him." Her eyes find mine. "Most of the time," she teased.

"Oh, sweetheart." I pin her to her back and she screams a little from the sudden attack. But as I kiss her, I feel her smile. As much as I love her pregnant with my babies, I can't wait until she's not. I miss sex and I hate feeling like she was so fragile.

CHAPTER TWENTY FIVE

I feel something cold on my legs and it's awkward enough to wake me. But as I wake up, I realize there's a pain. It's a dull ache, but a stabbing pain strikes and I can't catch the yelp that escapes. It's enough to frighten Leo awake.

"Sweetheart, what's..."

Leo pulls the sheets back and the wet spot in our bed is huge. It mirrors in his eyes when I glance his way. It's no secret that I was the one to wet the bed, but it means something different now than it did when I was two.

"Sweetheart, just relax. I'll get you to the hospital." His voice was a bit fearful and nervous, but the smile on his face was so huge. I know he's buzzing with excitement over this. Today's the day he really becomes a daddy, and he's going to have his hands full with a litter.

Leo disappears into the closet to get dressed and brings me back a hoodie to put on. "Good thing we repacked the baby bag yesterday." He goes to my dresser to get me a dry pair of underwear and helps me get decent enough to leave the house. I beg for him to let me take my slippers, but he insists on "real shoes". I see him packing them into the bag out the corner of my eye as we head out of the bedroom.

He leaves me on the doormat as he hurries down the street to get the car he borrowed from his parents. I had thought it was unnecessary, but a labor pain cripples me and I have to grab the doorframe to keep from collapsing. Why does it hurt so much! I feel my legs starting to give out from the amount of pain.

"Whoa, sweetheart."

Leo wraps his arms around my waist and helps me get to into the car. "It'll be okay, sweetheart. I promise. We'll get you to the hospital and they-eeoow!"

Until he screamed, I didn't realize how tightly I was squeezing his hand. "I'm so sorry, Leo." I can't seem to control that my emotions and I'm crying from having a "strong" moment.

"No, sweetheart, it's okay."

The more he tries to soothe me, the more the tears flow. A sharp jab hits and I scream so loud that he swerves the car, almost hitting a parked car.

"We-we're almost there, s-sweetheart."

I don't know who's more scared now, Leo or myself. I thought he'd be my rock. The one all reassuring and confident, but he's human just like me. I groan as he pulls up to the front of the hospital, leaving the car running. He helps me out, calling for help himself. My feet feel like lead and I just want to curl up at home in bed. A nurse comes and Leo's talking to her, but I don't know about what. All I can think about is the pain and trying not to fall. If I fall, I'll hurt our babies and I don't want to kill our babies again.

Leo kisses my forehead and pulls me into his chest as I scream out from another labor pain.

"I can't do this," I cry into his chest. It hurts so much that I wish someone would just kill me. "Leo, I can't."

He's rubbing my back, trying to calm me down, but it's not working this time. When the nurse comes with a wheelchair, there's almost a look of relief on his face. Like he doesn't have to put up with me now. Like he's finally rid of me. *Oh no, is he going to leave me?*

I try to get out of the wheelchair. I can't let Leo leave me. Not now! But the nurse puts her hand on my shoulder to keep me in the chair as she wheels me down hallway after hallway. It probably wouldn't even take her hand to keep me in the chair with the way these labor pains are hitting, and it feels like they're getting closer to each other.

The nurse is telling me things, but none of it registers. All I can think about is how Leo just left me...

I can still feel the pain, but it's more of an ache now. The only thing really bothering me is the dried up tears on my face. It feels like there's something there, even though I know there's not. I try to move my face to get rid of the feeling but all I do if make Leo laugh at me.

"The doctor said you're almost ready." He squeezes my hand gently.

I feel so stupid for having doubted him. Of course he had to go move the car, but I was too drugged up on the pain to see clearly. At least with the epidural and whatever they had dripping in my IV, I could at least think.

"Remember, Michael, Sam, and Ember. There's going to be two girls in there."

He chuckles. "I know sweetheart. Two *boys*," he teases.

The doctor comes back in. He's been back and forth quite a bit in the hour we've been here. I gave up caring the fourth or fifth time he checked to see how dilated I was.

"It looks like it's time." The doctor stepped into the hallway to call a couple nurses in. They pushed in a couple bassinettes and set them off to the side as they got cleaned up.

"Now I'm going to need you to push hard, Cat." He sat down between my legs at the end of the table. I could hear the wheels on his stool as he got closer. "I need you to get these babies out, okay? I'm only here to help and I need you to help me make sure they're okay."

A nurse came up next to me on the bed on the opposite side than Leo. She told him to hold my hand and let me squeeze it as I pushed. He had to be my focal point and try to keep me calm.

"Okay, Cat. Push!"

I tried, but it felt like I wasn't doing anything. The doctor kept telling me to push and Leo kept doing some stupid breathing thing. It felt like I was stuck. Like there was a plug between my legs that wasn't there before and it just hurt more as I tried to push.

I groaned. I cried. I squeezed Leo's hand. I pushed. I felt so tired when the doctor said the baby was crowning. Those words meant nothing, but I heard the doctor say I was going well and to keep pushing. The pressure just hurt so much and then it was gone.

I heard a wailing from somewhere in the room. *Was that me?* My eyes searched, somehow knowing it wasn't me but someone that now belonged to me. Leo had a smile on his face and his gaze was off towards the back of the room.

He smiled as he leaned down to whisper, "That's our little Michael."

"Mi-cha-el?" I felt so out of breath. All that work and only one?

Leo nodded and I heard the doctor telling me to push again. There was that pressure again, but it wasn't as bad this time. It came and went faster. Only this time, I didn't hear any screaming. Maybe that feeling wasn't what I thought it was.

"Samuel." Leo squeezed my hand a little. His face looked worried. There were hushed voices about a cord and a neck, but I couldn't make out what the nurse was saying.

Something was off, but I didn't have time to think. That pressure was back and it felt like whatever pain meds they gave me were wearing off. I felt tears stinging my eyes again as the doctor yelled at me for one last push.

It was dead silence again. My head just lolled to the side, trying to see through Leo. It seemed to take forever before I heard a little whining.

"Leo..." I wanted him to tell me about our babies. Where was Michael? Was Sam okay? Did we have a girl or were we going to fight over a third boy name?

I thought I was asking all my questions. That was when I realized that my world had gone black.

# CHAPTER TWENTY SIX

# Leo

There he was. Doctor Alden. He was the one to blame.

I pinned him to the wall when he came out of the scrub room. A growl rattled around my throat. "What the hell happened?!"

Cat was rushed away to the emergency room. Half my babies were dead. And none of them were with me right now. Cat had passed out and she hadn't woken up. Her hand had gone cold. I needed answers.

"Calm down, son." The man's hands were raised up in front of him. "We don't know what happened, but we're trying our best to keep your wife and children alive."

I hoped they were.

I crumbled.

"Your son and daughter are being cleaned and measured, and being kept safe. You'll be able to hold them soon."

"And what about my wife? You have to heal her and let me hold her too!" The look on his face just kept my panic rising. Why wasn't he reassuring me about Cat? She was my life. I needed her! I did this to her. She didn't want kids. I did this to her and now she was leaving me. Hot tears streamed down my face. That's why he wasn't talking about Cat. She was someone in this damn hospital dying. She was dying and I couldn't be there for her.

The doctor easily pushed me back and moved from the wall. "Sir, we're doing the best to help her but you have to let me go. I'm going to help her, and I can find more about what's going on."

He motioned for a nurse to fetch me. I didn't want to leave. I couldn't leave her. My heart was shredding, and I was being exiled to the waiting room lobby.

Michael snoozed in his basinet. He had been out when I was allowed into the nursery. Seeing my babies was all I had. How could half a day pass and there was no information? The nurse had taken pity on my sorry soul. I had stared in through the glass window at my little babies all morning. They looked so small. Hell, they were so small.

Ember was so tiny bundled up, or maybe I was just really big. Either way, she was perfect. "As beautiful as your mommy."

The memory choked me up. Cat had been tiny too. We had met when she was born. Now I had met our little ones, but she was gone. It didn't feel right to be here without her. The little one squirmed in my arms until she had her face snuggled right up against my chest. Just like her mom.

I promised that I would cry in front of my babies, but the tears stung my eyes already. What if Cat never got to hold our angels?

"Leo?"

The doctor's rougher voice stirred Ember and she started to fuss. "Shh, sweetie. It's okay. Daddy's here." It was so strangely wonderful how easy being a dad came, and she settled back down. "I'm Leo. Is it about my wife?"

The man nodded and I started to follow. "It probably best you leave the baby in the nursery. We may be a while."

Reluctantly, I handed off my little girl. It almost felt like being crushed by a glacier with how fast the emptiness of her little heat affected me. She fussed in the nurse's arms and the pull to rush back to her grew, but any word on Cat dulled that. I had to know about my love.

The doctor wouldn't come right out and admit she was dead, or what was wrong with her. He started to lead us on a walk around the building. "Her body went into shock," he finally said. "We have her stabilized, but she hasn't woken yet. We're not sure when that would be."

Cat was alive. It should have been a relief, but it wasn't. How could she not be awake yet?

"What does that mean? How does... Can't you make her get up?"

He shook his head. "Her body has slipped into something of a coma. We could force her to revive with medication, but it comes with a risk."

There was nothing more of a risk than letting her stay in a coma! She could slip away at any moment and I'd never get her back. She'd never get to hold our babies. "Do it." There was no choice here. I needed her back and whatever the risk was, it couldn't be the same bill for letting her stay in the coma.

"She's pregnant and she could lose the babies."

What? I couldn't have heard that correctly. "No, doctor," more like idiot, "she was pregnant. Cat gave birth to our babies this morning." What a joke. There was no way this place was going to help Cat. They thought she was still pregnant when clearly she was not. I had to get us all transferred to some place that had a clue about what they were doing.

"There were two pregnancies." The doctor nodded towards a work station and started to pull something up on the computer. "Your wife missed her last scheduled ultrasound because of the emergency she was admitted for. With the bleeding, they feared she was too fragile to put through the procedure."

The screen went dark and then a petite-frame outline lit up. I recognized it as an ultrasound, and that small body of the one I loved. There were three large lumps lit against the dark background. Two looked like a pair of boobs. "The two larger white lights and the reddish one just behind them are the litter Cat just birthed. But you can see," he hit a button and tiny ghost-like humps glided onto the screen, "a second pregnancy took."

I counted three tiny little bumps. There were three little babies of ours left. "How?" I wasn't sure how I managed to find my voice.

"Her menstrual cycle must have taken a few months to fully stop. In that time, you two must have engaged in intercourse and additional eggs were fertilized." It sounded so simple and harmless. I put two litters inside my love. Six babies that were all ours.

"Even if we had caught the second pregnancy on the ultrasound, I'm not sure we could have prevented her body from going into shock. Cat is a petite woman and her pregnancy was already classified as high-risk. We just would have been more prepared for this."

I doubted anything would have prepared for this. How could they really have stopped Cat from slipping into a coma and kept one of my boys alive?

"What now?" Would I get to see my love finally?

The doctor took a deep breath and sighed. "What do you value life?" I couldn't even understand that question. There was no way I could answer it. "Because your wife won't survive a second pregnancy."

Three lives that already have a piece of my heart or the love of my life?

I had to give up one.

How could I choose?

How could I live with myself?

# CHAPTER TWENTY SEVEN

# Leo

"Want to go say goodnight to mama?" It was finally getting easier to smile again at bedtime. It had to be Ember. She'd lay in bed talking to Cat for hours if I let her, but she'd always give us time alone too. Maybe it was her early maturity and understand how rough things were going for me, just by instinct, or maybe it was because she had so much of her mother in her that it didn't feel like I lost something.

She smiled and ran down the hall, opening the spare bedroom door. I watched as she ran to the side of the bed and pulled herself up. Ember slipped right into the groove between Cat's arm and body. It seemed the more days that passed, the less there was of Cat and the more there was of Ember.

I sat at the foot of the bed, resting my hand on her leg. I hoped somehow she knew we, I, was here. The monitor just beeped softly to let us know her heart was still beating. Sometimes I think I sit here just for the small reassurance of it. Most of the time though, at least with Ember, I listen to our daughter's life through her small eyes. She has so much of Cat in her.

That had been one thing I struggled with. Ember was born with my dark hair and blue eyes. When Cat slipped away, I hated our little girl for something she couldn't control, and at the time I didn't know her eyes would darken to the light chocolate color of Cat's. I had raised my wife, and now I was raising our daughter. And somehow, they were exactly the same and so different. I liked to think that somehow Cat was teaching her about life from wherever she drifted off.

"Did you tell mama it's almost your birthday?" *Four years, Cat. Our baby's growing up... without you.*

Ember shook her head and sat up on her knees to look at her mom. "Daddy says I'm going to be four and I get a cake." She looked back at me for approval. I smiled and watched her face light up. "That means I get a wish."

And I knew where this was going. It went the same way every year and for so many nights. For so many things she wanted her mom to be there. I want to run from the room so I can't hear it and have those words chip at my heart that's barely together.

"I wish you'd wake up, mama. Wake up for my birthday," she said softly. Ember starts to tell her about all the things she wants them to do when she wakes up.

I couldn't take it anymore. I can't take thinking about a future that would never come. Things we'll miss out on. A life without her. "Ember, give mama her goodnight kiss. We have to get you in bed."

Her face drops and I almost cave. It's like Cat's looking back at me and trying to persuade me into getting her an ice cream cone. I know I can't, and I'm relieved when Ember kisses her forehead and slips off the bed. Her tiny hand grabs onto mine and I try to keep it together as we leave Cat alone for another night. Another day we didn't have with her.

"Daddy, think mama will wake up this time?"

I lift her up on her bed and tuck her in. Anything to avoid answering that. I don't want to break her heart and tell her what the doctors said. I don't want her to know that her mom was never going to wake up and how selfish I was by keeping her alive like this. I don't want her to think about me killing her mom, my love, my Cat.

"I don't know, sweetie." It's the best I can do.

"I've been a good girl." She bites her bottom lip, as if waiting for me to confirm or deny that.

I get up and look to our overflowing bookcase for a story. I want to read her something happy. Something that could distract both of us. "I know you've been. You're daddy's little angel."

"Then she's going to wake up." I hear the resolve in her small voice. "She's going to eat cake with me and we'll do girly things, daddy."

I just crawl in bed next to her with the book. Maybe it was a bad idea to pick a princess book. At this point, it just feels like I'm giving Ember more ideas to get her hopes up. "Then she has to. That cake is going to be yummy and I know mama likes yummy cake."

I open the book to start our story and I can feel her eyes on me. Our little girl is like a sponge when it comes to the stories I have of Cat. I know she wants to ask to hear more, but she won't. She never does after I snapped at her once. It was just so hard doing this alone and dealing with what happened. Maybe one day, after Cat's gone and it doesn't feel so raw, I'll be able to tell her more. I want to be able to tell her more, tell her everything. I just can't right now. I feel her sigh and snuggle into my side. She's disappointed, but somehow I feel like she knows.

# CHAPTER TWENTY EIGHT

# Leo

*The house is on fire!*

It's the first thought I have when I hear the alarms going off. I stumble out of bed, only finding one slipper. Halfway down the hall to Ember's room, I realize there's no danger. The loud beeping is coming from the room across from hers. It reaches into my chest and seizes my heart.

"Daddy." She comes out of her room, teary-eyed. "Noisy."

Ember's rubbing her eyes as she comes to me to fix things. Only, I know this is the one thing I can't. That's Cat's monitor.

"It's alright, sweetie. Let's get you back in bed and I'll make it stop." Somehow my feet are moving again. One slipper after a foot, into her bedroom. It all feel surreal as I set her back in her bed.

It doesn't even feel like I'm walking, almost tripping over my unevenly covered feet. I need to know, but I don't want to know. I don't want to see my love's face distorted in pain. I don't want to hold her body and know she's left me forever this time. Slowly, I push open the door and I hear a raspy sound. *Oh god, she's suffocating!*

I have to wipe at my eyes just to see anything. My vision is so blurry that I can barely make out the bed from the rest of the room.

"L... e... o."

It's so faint that I doubt I heard anything. I finally lost it and my mind's playing tricks on me. It's trying to find a way for me to survive this, and I know I have to for Ember's sake, but right now I don't think I will. I hear it again, but it can't be what I so desperately hope for.

My hand finds the edge of the bed, but it's hers that finds me. I feel the weakest grip as her fingers try to meet mine. It can't be but, wiping my eyes again, I can see that hers are struggling to watch me. And she sees me crumbling. My arms wrap around her and everything, including that annoying alarm, disappears.

"D-daddy?"

I move back, just the slightest to see our daughter watching us. She's trying so hard to process everything. Ember hugs my side and peeks around me to see Cat. "It's okay, sweetie."

Finally I turn off the alarm and it feels eerily silent now. I smile at our little girl and then at Cat, but it falters. Her eyes say everything. I see the confusion, and for a moment the betrayal. She has no idea who Ember is.

"Sweetheart?" I try to get her attention, but it seems like she physically can't take her eyes off Ember. "Cat, this is Ember. Ember Rae." I smile, trying to reassure her when the name triggers her to glance my way. I'm gently rubbing Ember's back, knowing there has to be a million things in that little head of hers right now. "Ember, sweetie, meet your mama."

Two sets of eyes stare at me, one blue and the other brown. I know they want answers and are full of confusion, but I'm overflowing with happiness and trying not to drown them. I finally have my whole family back!

"Mama?" Ember sounds cautious. As if this person wasn't the same one she talked to and loved so much, just because she was awake now. I could see her looking for confirmation, just like she does with me, but Cat's so lost. Lost in knowing what was going on. Lost in knowing our daughter. So instead I nod and let Ember know she's right. She missed her birthday by a week, but her mom had finally woken up.

I dry my eyes, keeping them that way for a while, as Ember climbs up into bed like she does every night. It's hard to believe a handful of hours ago that Cat was still lost to us. I watch them both as they try to take each other in, Cat more so. I could only imagine how confusing it all was to her. To be giving birth one moment and then seeing your newborn as a little girl. Ember kissed her forehead, like she always does, and then snuggled next to her.

"I knew you'd wake up for my birthday, mama," she says quietly.

I lay in bed, just watching her. I spent the night with Cat in the spare bedroom. Maybe it was out of fear that she'd slip away or that I'd wake up and it all would have been a dream. But she's real and warm in my arms. Last night had taken quite a toll on all of us. Ember had fallen asleep shortly after and I had to carry her back to bed. It was the only time I left Cat's side. The questions had started as soon as her voice got sturdier with her words, but even the answers couldn't keep her awake for long.

It's hard to sleep when you're fearing someone won't wake up again. I had gone over how I would break the news to Ember that her mom died, passing away quietly one day when she went out to play. I had no idea how I'd tell her that Cat died now that she woke up. She surely wouldn't believe me and always be lingering onto the hope with no chance she'd see her mom again. I had to make sure that I didn't lose her again.

"Hey," I say softly, seeing her eyes open slowly. It takes a while for her eyes to adjust to the brightness of the dim morning light that creeps in around the curtain, and I seize the opportunity to kiss her forehead.

"Leo?" Her voice sounds unnaturally airy still, like she's not able to take a breath.

"Yes, sweetheart?" I watch as a smile tries to come on her face. It's stopped by something though and it leaves me feeling robbed and wanting.

Her eyes leave mine and I fight the urge to tilt her head up so she has to look at me. "Was that... is that really our baby?"

I had tried to fill her in last night, answering her questions, but she had fallen asleep. "Yes, that's our Ember Rae." I smile. Her hair is still so soft as I run my fingers through it and tuck a strand behind her ear.

"But our baby... should be a baby." I know she's still processing it all and struggling.

"She was four years ago, sweetheart. You gave birth and I thought I lost you, but you slipped into a coma." And I did lose her. I almost gave up on us. "I know you don't remember but, Cat, it's the truth. That's our little girl and you have no idea how much she loves you. Every night she crawled in bed and told her about her day. Every night she'd give you a kiss goodnight and I had to drag her to bed." I smiled softly and let that all sink in.

"What about Michael and Sam?" Cat asked softly. It seemed that her voice was getting stronger the more she woke up. But I still didn't want to tell her, no matter how strong she seemed. Cat was going to be upset, but I wasn't sure if she had it in her after learning what happened to her and Ember. Her eyes are watching me and the longer I take to answer, the more I can see her mind worry and work to exaggerate stories.

"Sam was stillborn." I figured that would be the best way to start, seeing as Cat was still conscious then. Saying it out loud, and hearing it myself, makes it feel too real. "Michael didn't make the night. The doctor thought it was something with his lungs. That he swallowed too much fluid during birth and couldn't get it all out."

She buries her face into my chest so that I won't see her cry, but I feel my shirt growing wetter. All I can do is gently rub her back and be here for her as she accepts it. I had four years to come to term with it, Cat was barely awake for twelve hours.

"He had this mess of blonde hair, sweetheart. And wail... I thought you were a noisy baby, but you had nothing on Michael." I'm not sure why I keep talking. Maybe it's to distract myself from joining her, and maybe it's because I'd want to know about our babies if I had been in her place. "Sam and Ember had my dark hair." I leave out how sickly blue he looked when the doctor passed him by to the nurse to hurry out. I had thought my world ended when we lost our son, but I had no idea what world-ending really was.

"She had these sky blue eyes, and I hated that she looked just like me. All I could think about after you slipped away was how I wanted a piece of you. Ember was all I had left. You know I never finished the baby book." I had given up when Cat miscarried our last litter. It was too hard to read about children when we lost ours. The book got shoved somewhere or packed up in a box buried in the closet. "I didn't know eyes and hair could change color as they got older. I was so happy when her brown eyes came out. There's no doubt she's your daughter. I kept telling myself you were looking out for her wherever you were and teaching her. Just the way she'd look at me and how she acts reminded me of you every day."

Cat pulls back a little to peek up at me. Her eyes are so puffy and red, but she couldn't look more beautiful to me. Seeing her alive made every other idea of beauty seem miniscule. I don't regret telling her about our children and I can see through her pain that she doesn't either. I wrap my arms around her and hold her as she rests her head on my chest.

"Daddy?"

Ember's standing in the doorway, wearing her pink starry pajamas. Her eyes drift between me and her mom. I know this is what she always wished for and the change has to be hard on her too, even if it's a good change.

"Why don't you come and keep mama company while I make us some breakfast?" There's a smile creeping on her face as she scurries over and up onto the bed. I feel Cat's grip on me tighten for a moment and I don't even think that she might see Ember as a stranger pushing her love expectations on her. But she slowly moves and sits up against the headboard, letting the little girl snuggle up next to her.

I smile weakly as I watch them. My family's complete, but it's not whole. It was going to take some time before we got to where we thought we would be. Heading to the door, the anxiety over leaving my wife and the fear of something happening is almost crippling. Cat manages a faint smile when she glances up and sees me staring. My family is complete, but there's still work ahead to make our family feel like one. I listen for a moment as Ember starts talking about her dream with a unicorn and purple poodle before I head to the kitchen. My mind can't help but think of the foods that will steal me away from Cat the least          amount          of          time.

CHAPTER TWENTY NINE

# *Leo*

I stare up at the doctor as he gives Cat the same speech again. I had wanted to keep her all to myself that first week but it was time to start living again, for all of them. There was no way to describe her parents reaction when they saw her, and their threat to keep her there a few days seemed more like a promise that I didn't even want to risk leaving to use the bathroom. The only one not happy was Ember. She wanted her mom all the time, not that I could blame her, but there were tests and doctor visits now and they agreed not to let their daughter see that.

The doctor leaves and Cat moves to change out of the paper medical gown. "Let me help you with that, sweetheart." I get up and cross the room. Standing alongside the table seat, I untie the back and can't help but really notice how thin she became. It wasn't like she was that big to start off with, not even during the pregnancy.

Cat doesn't fight me as I fuss over her. That fight was one we already had. It upset her so much that I had to catch her before her legs gave out and carry her to bed, lying to Ember that her mom was just really wanted to take a nap. It was hard to see my strong wife so fragile, and fussing over her was the only way I knew how to care for her, all the while hoping she'd completely return to me.

"Thanks, Leo." Her voice is soft. It's not like those first few days when she woke up. It just seems to be her new volume, and she can't speak louder than this. I kiss her as gently as her voice sounds and help her off the table and into the wheelchair. That was another unpleasant new change. The doctors thought it was something we should expect and take as normal. It was the same after each visit and test. She was in a coma and her body had to learn to be strong again. It was just a matter of time. She was doing well for someone who came out of such a long coma. That was all they said so they didn't have to say she wasn't getting better.

I wheel her down the hall and towards the car. Cat's been staring at her legs the whole time and I know she's dying to try walking again. The doctor said they could start thinking about physical therapy in a few weeks, as long as she was still improving or rather not getting worse.

She wraps her arms around my neck as I transfer her into the car and buckle her up. I kiss her cheek as she thanks me. That's another thing I don't fuss about. It's not worth fighting to tell her there's no need to thank me. Cat's my wife and I love her so very much. Having her in my life is all I need as thanks. I get behind the wheel and she's still acting strangely.

"Leo, can we talk about our baby?"

It takes me a little off-guard that she needs to ask. "Of course, sweetheart. What do you want to talk about?" Her hand comes over to hold mine on the shifter. Red flags are definitely going up.

"I want to talk about her binding," she says softly. It's not just quiet because her voice has become weak. It's quiet because I can see her cheeks redden slightly from embarrassment. What was there to be embarrassed about?

"You're going to have to be a little more specific than that. I mean, she's just four. It's not like we're marrying her off tomorrow." Or was that what she wanted to talk about? Had Cat married off our daughter between checking in for the appointment and leaving?

"I know." I feel her thumb gently run back and forth over my hand. "It's just... I want her to have what we have, Leo. I want her to know what love is."

I try not to laugh. I know she's being serious. "Sweetheart, she knows love. I love her and you love her."

"I didn't mean it like that. I want her to have someone she can love and loves her now. I never had to worry about how you felt or if I was going to like the guy my parents picked out. And you always made me feel loved. I just... I want that for our daughter."

I know what she means and now I'm starting to understand. It's less of doing it and more about the idea of it. This was a decision our parents had made and now it was ours. Would we arrange things for Ember how they were for us or go back to how the rest of the world did things? I gave her hand a gentle squeeze. "I think we should let her pick, but maybe in a couple years. I want our little girl to stay our little girl for a little while longer."

I turned off the highway and started to head towards her parents' house to pick up Ember. She's been oddly silent again. Cat's been looking out the window as I drove, and I can't get a good reading off her face. I know there's more she wants to say. After being asleep for years, there must be something she was thinking about.

"Something on your mind?" I ask softly.

Her eyes look so clear and bright as she looks at me. I swear those little flecks of gold in them twinkle. "I want to make love to you."

She states it clear as day, but it's like a foreign language to me. I have no idea how to respond to that. Well, no idea how to say it that wouldn't end up in a fight.

"Leo, we could stop at home or you could park the car." Cat starts, breaking the tension-filled silent air. "I want to have sex with you."

That last bit was the firmest I've heard her voice in a long time, and yet there's a hint of something I hadn't heard in years. She sounds like a little kid trying to get their way and I know, with this, that's exactly what she's trying to do. We both know there's no way we can have sex. She's not healthy enough for that yet. I do the only thing I can do. I avoid it and buy myself a little time until we get to her parents.

"Sweetheart, we're here already." I pull a smile to my face as I park the car in the driveway. I know she's upset with me, but there's no way I'm going to hurt her. She means way too much to me. It's not that I don't want to have sex with her, and I know how she's struggled with it before. It's that I have to forget all that and be the bigger adult in the relationship right now.

She pulls her hand from mine and crosses them in front of her. "Sweetheart," I try softly to get to her to look at me. "Cat."

I reach for her and she all but jumps out of the car, not that she physically could. I sigh and rest my head against the back of my seat. "I want to so badly, trust me. I just don't think it's a good idea right now. You need to be resting and getting better."

"What if I can't get better?" It was barely a whisper, but it sounded like loudest thing on the planet. It was the fear we both had and were afraid that if we said it aloud that it would become real.

# CHAPTER THIRTY

# Leo

I pour milk into Ember's cereal bowl while she watches me from her booster seat at the table. "Okay, daddy. That's good."

She smiles up at me while I yawn. Lately, I've been a zombie until I've had at least three cups of coffee in me. I brush her bangs back as she dips some cartoon character shaped cereal prize spoon into her breakfast. I watch her to make sure she's not going to make a mess, until I hear Cat's stomach growl. For some reason, she was insisting on waiting until Ember was taken care of and had just been sipping her juice.

"I should get those eggs going." My smile feels lazy and half-assed in my sleepy state, but Cat just smiles up at me. I can see it in her eyes, what she's thinking, and I know that look. It's the look she got, before the pregnancies, when she wanted to jump my bones. She'd always say I looked too sexy not to, and I know she's trying to keep herself in check. There's no way she'd say something like that in front of our daughter. I think it's less of trying to keep her innocent mind innocent and more of Cat not wanting to have the sex talk and explaining things.

I can feel her eyes watching me as I move about the kitchen to get our breakfast going. It makes me a bit self-conscious as I bend over to get the eggs out of the bottom drawer in the fridge. Cat wants me to sleep with her and I know she's trying to convince me that I want to do it just as badly. There's nothing more that I want to do. I know it's horrible to think, but I'm glad she can't move her lower half. Her hands alone at night in bed are hard enough to contain. If she ever straddled me, there wasn't anything in the world that would stop me from being with her. And I was pretty sure she knew that. Pointing out my morning wood and commenting how it was a waste not to use it was getting harder to ignore.

"So what do my beautiful girls want to do today?" I ask, cracking a few eggs into a bowl to whisk for scrambled eggs.

"The park?" Ember tries to ask with a mouthful of cereal. A bit of the milk escapes, but Cat's already wiping that up. It came so easily for her, being a mom. After the shock and loss of the years, it was like things should have been.

I grabbed a pan to heat up on the stove while I finished beating the eggs. "I don't know, sweetie." The park was better than yesterday's beach suggestion. There were quite a few places I could push a wheelchair, but I didn't want Cat getting bored by going to the same places over and over.

"I think the park's a great idea, Ember." Just the way Cat said that gave me impression that our girl's spirit had dropped. "I'm sure we can convince daddy to save some slices of bread so we can feed the ducks."

"Yay! Daddy," I can hear the smile back on her face without looking to see it. "Can we save bread?"

I chuckle as I push around the eggs. "Oh, I don't know." Ember begs again, and even Cat. "I guess. But you have to finish breakfast and get dressed. No sitting in front of the TV all day. Understand?"

I hear laughter. Oh god, it's her laugh. It feels like ages since I heard it. It doesn't seem like Cat laughs enough lately. Well, at least for my tastes. I grab one big plate for the eggs and two forks. Another thing that seems less is her appetite, but the doctors say it could just be a side effect of her medications. It just seemed easier to dirty only one plate, and this way Cat wasn't feeling hard on herself for not eating much. She probably knew I ate more of our shared helpings, but it was a little harder to prove.

As I brought over the plate, I watched with a smile as our daughter slipped off her booster and went to hug her before running to her room to get dressed. "Ganging up on me now?" I push the empty cereal bowl to the side to make room for the plate of eggs. "What am I going to do with you, sweetheart?" I chuckle and take a bite.

"I don't know. Guess you'll have to sell me," she jokes. There's no way I'd ever do that. Cat pokes the eggs a little and gives it away when she bites her bottom lip. "I think we should take Ember to the zoo."

I swallow my bite before I speak. "Today? I thought we all just agreed on the park."

"I was thinking for her birthday. You know, let her see the animals."

"Cat, her birthday's like eight months away." My body wants to laugh, but something just feels off. I can't really put my finger on it, but most of the time this feeling comes when Cat starts talking about our daughter. I don't know if it's because she feels like she needs to try to out-do herself as a mom or because something bad is going to happen. It has to be her trying to make up for lost time, because the doctors haven't said anything.

"Leo, do you remember your first transformation?" Cat asked quietly. She still hasn't taken a bite and it worries me a little more than what's going on in her mind.

"I turned into a turtle." This time I let myself laugh. As far as the choice for first animal, it's a horrible one. It was something I got teased about for years, until people found out about the arrangement with Cat. Kids were supposed to be great things like dogs or horses or birds. A turtle was boring and useless. "It's hard to forget something like that."

She reaches over and takes my hand, abandoning the fork. Cat doesn't need to say it, she knows it had to be hard on me and I can see how much she loves me. I never told her before. Not because I was trying to hide it, but because she never asked. It wasn't so much as a genetic risk where we had to worry about what Ember would turn into first and if some car would end up running her over.

"Do you remember my first?" She smiles softly up at me.

"Of course, sweetheart. You were the cutest little black and white cat I ever saw. At first you were all confused, but then you curled up on my lap and ended up falling asleep." Her fur had been so soft. That was the first time she ever slept with me. Well, the first we slept together. I had ended up falling asleep after being trapped by her on my lap and bored to death by the animated kid movie.

"I know she can pick anything." Her voice goes quiet as she moves back. Her fingers toy with the fork and I'm really debating feeding her myself. "I just thought that maybe she could have a special first. I mean, I have nothing against what we picked and what our friends picked. I just want her to have options and the best we can give her."

"Sweetheart." She finally looks back up at me. There's something working its way inside her head and I can see it in her eyes. I don't like how it has taken the sparkle out of them. Cat doesn't say anything and it starts to eat at me again. What is going on with the woman I love? I lean over the table and kiss her.

"Leo, please, make love to me."

This time I don't reject her meek voice. I nod and kiss her again.

# CHAPTER THIRTY ONE

# Leo

"Ember, come on, you're going to be late for the bus!" I sigh as I head back down the hall to our bedroom. I don't understand it. How can my handicapped wife be up and dressed before our little girl even got out of bed?

She manages to slowly roll herself over and take my hand. "Calm down, Leo. It won't be the end of the world. You'll just have to drive her to school if she misses."

That's what Cat doesn't understand. It could be the end of the world. It would mean leaving her alone for half an hour as I drove our girl there and came back, longer if traffic was bad. I used to drive Ember all the time on my way in to work but, since Cat's wakening, I haven't. There's just too much that could happen while I was gone and she needed me now more than our daughter. I listen to little feet running around and try to focus on the gentle way Cat's rubbing the back of my hand.

"We've waited four years. What's an hour or two more?"

I sigh. She's right. She's always right. We had decided that we'd wait until Ember was at school so we could take our time and enjoy each other. There really wasn't much of a choice when all the activity of the day zapped what energy Cat had.

"Maybe even make it a sleep over at grandma and grandpa's?" Cat smiled innocently, but I know what she was trying to do. And I was completely falling for it.

"You know, I think I love you," I teased. I leaned down and kissed her. Only Cat could make me feel this way and I wanted to find a way to love her more, because loving her with all my heart didn't seem enough.

"Ew!" I laugh, hearing Ember. The face she has on is priceless. "Mama, no! Daddy has cooties!"

It seems like that is the new thing she picked up at school. I much prefer that over to the kids picking on her and saying she had a dead mom. It gutted me to hear her tell Cat that one of the nights before bed. She had curled up at her side and those tiny hands were clinging on for dear life. I had called the school, leaving a horrible voicemail message, but there was nothing they could do but talk to the class. Without Ember saying who was telling her these things, there was nothing the teachers could do but keep an ear open and stop what they heard. It seemed like everything got worse for a while because of what I had done. None of the kids would play with her, her best friend had barely talked to her. But all that was in the past now, and everything was going to be perfect.

"Okay, sweetie, we have to hurry." I grab her hand and hurry her out to the bus stop. She laughs, thinking I look funny and I bet that I do. Once Ember is on that bus, I'm the one that gets to be that horny teenager again or the kid with the new shiny toy. Cat's waiting for me and I want her. All of her, and the best part is that I finally get her again.

I kiss the top of Ember's head. "Have a good day at school." She's embarrassed, I can tell. She hurries in line and starts up the starts. "Try to learn something, sweetie. You're going to need to teach mama!" I laughed, crossing my arms over my chest. That last bit always seems to bright her day. Ember loves her so much. And right now, I want to love her quite a bit more.

I fidget a little, rocking back and forth on my feet, until the bus turns around the corner and out of sight. Shifting into a fox, I dart back inside and down the hall to where Cat wheeled herself to. Leaping onto her lap, I sit up and lick her cheek. That laugh is the sweetest music I ever heard.

"Leo!" She giggles and tries to stop me from slobbering all over her face with my wet foxy kisses.

Jumping on the bed, I stretch out and turn back. "Yes, sweetheart?" The smirk on my face must say it all. She just blushes and shakes her head, like she could get the naughty thoughts out of her head now. I wiggle my eyebrows and crawl over to her.

"You're ridiculous. You know that, right?"

She giggles as I leaned over and kiss her before getting off the bed. "Yes, but you still love me." And Cat beams at me. I can see it so clearly in her eyes how much she does. Before she can say anything, I kiss her. I don't want words right now. I just want to show her.

My hands slip around her gently and I lift her out of the wheelchair. It's come easy now after doing it for a few months. I lay her down softly on our bed, smiling down at her.

My fingers doodle shapes on her arm. Mostly loops and circles, not that I'm paying much attention. I can't help but think of all the times we've had together. There's not a second I'd change of our lives, except maybe her coma. I have been lucky. To think I doubted what we had in my teens and after we got married during the "no sex" decree. I had learned that sex with Cat was just the icing on the cake, not the cake.

She hadn't woken up yet, even though it was already mid-morning. Lately, Cat had been sleeping in, unless Ember slipped by me before I could get her on the school bus. Today, I'd like to think that it was my doing. That I had rocked her world so hard that I put her in a love-induced coma.

Not that I should be joking about a coma, even in my head. I hear her groan quietly, trying to fight waking, and I almost don't want her to get up, but it reassures me that she's alright. I loved having her head rest on my bare chest with those petite fingers splayed next to her face, like she was trying to keep me from escaping this slice of heaven.

Her eyes slowly fluttered open. "Morning, sweetheart," I spoke softly, knowing she wasn't awake just yet.

With a groan, Cat tries to bury her face into my chest. I can't help but chuckle at my wife's futile efforts. She should know I wouldn't let her fall back asleep. I was selfish that way – wanting every second of her time.

"Come on, sweetheart." I look to the alarm clock to let her know what time it is. Usually that's enough to get her moving, but I must have worn her out more than I thought. "How about I go make up lunch and we'll eat in bed?"

She nods a couple times before reaching blindly for the pillow, pulling it to her chest. I smile and shake my head at her as I get out of bed and look for my briefs. I pull them in before leaning over to kiss her cheek.

"I'll be back soon," I warn her softly.

# CHAPTER THIRTY TWO

I try not to move, mostly because I don't want to let go of Leo. But the pain is already back. In the last few days, it has gone from a constant dull ache to a stabbing pain. I know Leo's expecting more of me, but I don't care what time it is. Hunger is the furthest thing from my mind right now. While I know it wasn't a good idea, I don't regret last night with him at all. I know it will be our last. I've just been having this horrible feeling that our time was running out.

I roll over and latch onto the first thing I touch. The pain is getting worse. I almost wish someone was stabbing me. At least then there was something I could do. With this, whatever it was, I was helpless. I don't say anything, scared I'd end up yelling out in pain. I don't want Leo to know how badly it hurts. I don't want him to take me to the hospital again. I've already lost too much time away from my family.

By the time he gets back, I've managed to sit up against the headboard. My legs feel weak and achy from moving so little. I had kept the pillow against my chest, less for modesty and more for comfort when the pain strikes. I smile, but it feels forced and must look it.

"It's not that bad." Leo rolls his eyes. He has no idea. "If I wore you out that much, I'll let you nap while I go pick up Ember from your parents'."

We had decided that mine would watch her. It seems like they stayed away, not wanting to see and remember me like that. And it had to be hard, if what Leo says is true, to see a little girl that has so much of me in her. I think about her and wonder how the sleepover went while Leo climbs into bed with the tray.

"I made scrambled eggs, toast and those veggie sausage links Ember's addicted to." A mischievous grin takes over his face. For a moment I think he's scheming a way to sneak sex in before picking up our girl. Instead, he just takes a bite out of one of them. "Promise not to tell her. She'd kick me in the shins if she found out I gave them away. Even to you, I'd bet."

I can't help but keep smiling. I had no idea what the things were until Ember pulled them out of the freezer to show me what she was asking to have for breakfast.

And I had no idea a thing existed. Probably something new that came out during the years I missed. At least it was healthy.

"Thanks, Leo." My voice feels so unsure. I know he would be all over me like white on rice if it wasn't for my recovery stage, as the doctor called it. It hardly felt like I was recovering anything.

Even my hands still are a little shaky as I try to take a bite. Leo takes my fork and feeds me mouthful of delicious warm egg clouds without even needing to be asked. For only a moment do I feel like I've ruined a perfect man's life, but it's gone before I can really think it. It's like nothing can get me down because, in the grand scheme, it's not important at all. I rest my head on his shoulder and let him feed me a while longer.

"Your food's going to get cold," I say quietly. While I know that's true, I secretly don't want him to stop.

Leo laughs softly. "Sweetheart, I actually ate while I made yours. I didn't want you to worry about me and not eat. You know that you aren't eating enough lately."

And not only is that true, but it's perfect. I try to punch his arm, but it just ends up being a light tap that makes my hand ache more than the damage I probably did to him. "Stop being perfect, mister," I say. My eyes are starting to water up just thinking about how much better his life would be without having met. Leo would probably have a few litters, a beautiful blonde wife, and got promoted a few times. Instead, he's with me and our one baby from two litters, dusty straw-colored hair wife, and taking disability leave to take care of me. And for what? I'm just going to die.

I'm... I'm going to *die*.



Ember's been attached to my side the whole day. At first, I thought it was something my parents said or something that happened during her sleepover. But it was just that four years without a mom was too long and she didn't want to waste any more time. I was starting to wonder if they were teaching mindreading in school now, because that was exactly what I was doing. Both with her, and with Leo.

There wasn't much I could do with her or teach her. She was a little too young for anything I could pass on, and this darn wheelchair got in the way. The pain's always there and once Ember crawled onto my lap and just hit a bad spot. It took almost an hour to get her to stop crying, thinking she had hurt me and I was going to leave her. I don't even worry about Leo noticing the aspirin are slowly disappearing. For some reason, I don't care, even if I have to tell him the truth now.

"Mama, does this one go here?"

Ember holds up one of the puzzle pieces for me to see. It's an edge piece and the part of the lion matches up to where she wants to put it.

"I'm not sure, sweetie. Let's look at the box."

She moves a little on my lap as she reaches for the box and stares intently at it. Leo's been pretty intent on teaching her what the animals are, which just makes her more excited to go to the zoo for her birthday in a few months. Ember already know most of the animals on the puzzle – elephant, lion, giraffe, zebra – at least most of the time when she's not in a rush to name them.

"It looks like that was the lion's paw." I smile a little, seeing her hands holding the box. She must have set down the puzzle piece and now it was laying amongst the ten other pieces left to be added. "Sweetie, where's the puzzle piece?"

She glances up at me for a moment and then to her hands. It's amusing to watch the gears turns, and I know she's wondering where it went. Ember looks to me, confused and maybe thinking I stole it.

"I think you put it down, sweetie. Can you find it?" Ember ditches the box and looks for the piece that she just had in her hand.

"And what are my beautiful girls up to?" Leo walks by on his way to the kitchen with his bowl of popcorn kernels.

"Puzzle, daddy!" Ember bounces a little as she holds up a piece to show him.

"You know it's almost bedtime." And the pout's back. My little girl sure learned fast how to wrap Leo around her finger. Only, since I've been awake, it hasn't worked as well when it meant he'd have to share me. And I'm pretty sure that's how he's thinking too.

"Come on, daddy," I tease, taking Ember's side. At least for now. "We're almost done."

"Yeah, almost done," Ember repeats.

"Just ten more pieces left of our twelve piece animal puzzle."

"Animals."

He's amused. I'm sure he never thought he'd be ganged up on like this. Or maybe it is how adorable Ember is being, between her repeating and that pout.

"Nope, come on. Bedtime, sweetie." Leo gets up and holds his arms out for her, but she turns and buries her face into my chest.

"I want mama to read me a story."

Leo sighs, knowing he's fighting a losing battle.

"It's okay." I smile softly at him. I know he thinks I'm pushing myself, but I want to be a mom. I hadn't known before how right it felt. Like somehow this was what I was supposed to do with my life, who I was supposed to be. "I'll read you a story tonight. Why don't you go get your pajamas on and pick one out?"

I'm not sure if that little face could hold a bigger smile. I wince a little as Ember climbs off my lap to run to her bedroom, and it doesn't go unnoticed by Leo.

"Sweetheart, you should relax, head to bed." He crouches down next to me. "I know you're not feeling the best. You don't have to pretend to be Superman."

"Who?"

He chuckles and kisses my cheek. "Maybe Ember can fill you in on that reference. She likes my old comics more than you did," he teases.

Leo pushes me down to her room and she's standing in front of her little bookcase, trying to pick a book. I don't doubt she's heard all of them a few times over the years. Some look more worn on the spine than others. While Leo sets me in her bed, she manages to pick one. It's one of those with a broken in spine.

Ember runs over and jumps in bed to snuggle up with me. "Mama, I want this one."

She smiles and holds it out for me. It's a story my mom used to read when I was a kid, and I wonder if that's how my daughter got the book. Opening the cover, I see that it is the exact same book. It's hard not to smile at that.

"Okay," I wrap an arm around her and settle in for story time, "Once upon a time..."

Leo nudges me a little and reluctantly I wake up. It felt so good to doze off for a moment. After the story Ember hadn't quite fallen asleep yet, and it turned into Leo and I reminiscing about our childhood and adventures.

"Come on, sweetheart. It's your bedtime now."

He helps me get free from our daughter and back in the chair before tucking her in. I catch him yawning as we head to our bed. I tilt my head back, just to see him. I try to remember if he looked this handsome when I was a kid and this was the angle I saw him. Leo catches me smiling and leans down to kiss me as we pull up to the bed.

"I hope that wasn't my goodnight kiss," I tease.

It doesn't feel like my body's aching so much tonight. I watch him change and get ready for bed. I can't help but wonder if I could convince him to strip down and make love tonight. At the same time, I want nothing more than to wrap my arms around him and have him all to myself.

# CHAPTER THIRTY THREE

# Leo

"Oh, it's not, sweetheart."

I winks and crawl in bed. My arms pull her closer to me and I love the feeling of her being so close. I can feel the warmth and love we have for each other. I lean down to steal a kiss before she rests her head over my heart.

"Goodnight, sweetheart."

"'Night, Leo."

I feel her breathing slow down and guess that she's fallen asleep. It's been a while since she's slept without being in pain or constantly uncomfortable. I feel myself finally drifting off when I hear a soft trace of a voice.

"I love you, Leo."

The bed feels cold. Did Cat get up without me? She hadn't tried since the day she fell and I got the wheelchair. Nope. I feel her still in bed with me, but she's cold. Did I leave the window open last night? It had been so nice lately that it was a shame not to open them up and get some fresh air in this house. But it's not that. I can see the window is closed, and I'm not actually cold.

"Sweetheart?"

She doesn't move, but that's not unusual. Cat's been having a harder time sleeping and she's usually snoozing the morning away. It's when I go to gently shake her awake that I feel how cold she is. It wasn't the bed that was cold. It was my love in my arms.

"Cat, get up."

I shake her a little less gently. I think my heart knows, but my head doesn't want to believe it.

"Sweetheart, get up!"

I shake her so hard that her small body bounces off the bed. Every moment she doesn't wake up sprouts more tears until everything is a blur. I don't want to stop shaking her. I don't want to give up.

Cat's so still and cold, even when I clutch her against my body. I don't feel her warmth. I don't feel her heart. It's like there's a stranger in my bed, but it's just an empty version of Cat instead.

"Sweetheart... Cat..." Words are getting lost and what I have managed to get out are choking me up.

I hear Ember moving about in her room. I know I don't want our girl to come running in to find her mom like this. Hell, I don't want her to know at all. Reluctantly, I let Cat out of my arms and I'm crushed the instant I feel both warmer and colder by moving from her dead body. But I have to lock the door now, even though my legs don't feel strong enough to take a single step.

I crawl right back in bed once the deed is done. I'm going to have to call her parents to tell them, and maybe beg them to come and help with Ember. I feel so helpless when I know there was nothing I could have done to save my love.

"Mama? Daddy?"

I hear her little hand trying so hard to open our door. And I breakdown even more. I weep into Cat's chest, begging her to come back to me again and telling her over and over again how much I love her.

"I love you, Cat."

"Sweetheart, I love you so damn much."

# Epilogue

"Hey, mom."

I brush off some of the autumn leaves atop her stone. I can't believe she's been gone for so long. It really makes me think when I'm almost as old as she was when she died.

When dad told me her story, I struggled with it so much. It probably had to do with the fact that I heard it right after getting pregnant. Dad always did have rotten timing. It wasn't so much as accepting that my birth probably caused the coma or thinking that day in the park feeding ducks gave her a cold or something. It was that they had wanted my life to start and end with love like my mom's life had. Only difference between our stories so far was that I got to pick my husband and I've dealt with teasing and bullying because dad wasn't following tradition. Sure the super hot guy I was crushing on didn't have understanding parents to put what could have been love first, but I don't regret it. I ended up with a husband that I love to pieces.

"Max did it again," I joke, running a hand over my huge belly. "The doctor thinks it is twins this time and he's willing to bet next time it's going to be triplets."

Carefully, I sit down on the grass. My jeans might get a little damp but the sweater was long enough to cover my butt. Besides, you can never put a price on mother-daughter time.

"I was hoping he'd wait a little longer so Ella could actually be helpful. We tried to bake dad a cake for his birthday and she *insisted* on helping. I think there was more flour on us than in that cake."

Mom would have loved Ella and probably, together, drove dad insane. It's hard, still, not to blame and hate her for leaving us and not having these kinds of times with my kids.

"Dad's finally doing better. He doesn't wake up screaming anymore." I knew what might have kept replaying in his nightmares.

"Max has been trying to get him out fishing. You know, get him out doing something. And Ella's been teaching him how to dance when they watch the morning cartoons." I can't help but laugh just picturing those two. "Poor dad has no rhythm." And my little girl is not shy about telling him.

"Ember?"

I turn just moments before a silly grinned mob of hair runs into me.

"Mama!" She's giggling as she flops over with me.

"Hey, monkey. I thought you and grandpa were going to feed the ducks."

"She threw the slices of bread in the water before I could break off pieces." Dad sighs and sits with the rest of us. "I thought you had errands to run."

"I did, but I wanted to stop and tell mom about the babies before I picked up my monkey."

"Yea, she'd be upset if you didn't tell her yourself." He sighs. "I can't believe she's gone. It still feels like yesterday she was walking you to the bus and..."

I reach over and hug him when I hear dad getting choked up. It's not long before Ella feels left out and tries to squirm in between us. She's what puts a smile back on his face... at least for a little while.

Coming Soon...

# Chapter One

Ava's death was just another suicide on the fourth page of the newspaper. It fit in inconspicuously amongst the other deaths which included old age and one other suicide, in the form of an overdose. It made her out to be just another overworked young woman who gave into the everyday troubles that ultimately resulted in taking her own life. But for the dark haired man that stood a few feet behind her family, watching the casket being lowered into the ground and out of his sight, he knew suicide was the last thing she'd do. And maybe because of that, the news had come as such a shock and the matter of her remains dealt with so quickly. The sting of her sudden departure screamed to be hidden beneath the earth.

Jack Havest had known the auburn haired firecracker for just over three years. He had been working on figuring out a better way to increase the lifespan of rail when she stopped by his cubicle. But for some reason as she stood there next to his superior as they were introduced, there was a feeling that they just had to know each other and the others hurrying around the office disappeared for a moment.

It hadn't taken long to befriend Ava Koltrin. At first, the meetings near her cubicle down the hall were slightly awkward. She had to think he was just another creeper the way he'd peek his head over the cubicle wall. He had tried to be sneaky about it and he'd walk in after seeing she was there. But that seemed to have changed quickly before the week was over. She was easy to talk to, even if she was more reserved in her choice of words. But there was something about her that made Jack want to tell her everything. And that was something that hadn't dissipated over the years.

Their harmless chit-chat had turned into lunches and into working as close to each other as possible. Looking back now, it was funny to think that a few of the older men in the department had pegged them as a couple long before they had even thought about it themselves. Ava had admitted later that one particular old man had started to tease her a few days after she started work. Of course she thought he was just a crazy old gossip who was trying to get her goat.

For Jack it had been nothing but suspicious looks when they were seen talking to each other, even if it was for a moment or simply saying good morning as they passed each other in the hall. He had just decided that they were still not used to seeing a new person around the office. Being a friendly co-worker was the excuse he had used a few times to calm things back down and to stop Ava from catching on. It wasn't until later that Ava had told him about the sly comments that were mentioned within earshot or hinted at that he failed to notice. He had laughed it off knowing most of them already and raising an eyebrow at some he hadn't heard.

The hand of Ava's father on his shoulder as the aging man passed with down-trotted eyes snapped Jack out of his thoughts of those earlier, happier times. The two shared a moment of painful understanding before leaving Jack alone next to the grave. They had both lost someone dear. Someone who wouldn't let herself be easily replaced, even if that was possible. There was no one near as special as she had been. Maybe if the technology ever became advanced enough to merge people together. But then it was still debatable.

Even though he was alone with Ava now, he couldn't urge his feet to take him nearer to her. The body in that wooded box wasn't the girl he knew. That person was a cold shell of a lively person. Although the funeral had been closed casket, the scene inside couldn't have been a pleasant one. There was no way anyone would want to remember her that way. And no one except those who dealt with or heard the gossip of fatalities knew what she probably looked like now.

Instead of accepting the fact that she broke her promise to never leave him, he couldn't let her go nor go to her now. It was just like those first few months. Like forbidden fruit in the Garden of Eden. The temptation drawing you close while the pain lurking in the nearby shadows. Ava would always cling to his thoughts as long as he lingered in this town or clung to the things they enjoyed. Like their hot cocoa movie nights.

But the pain of returning to work tomorrow and feeling her absence again was more tolerable than staring at the hole in the ground. As Jack turned to head towards his car parked on the side of the road, the forgotten cell phone in his dark suit's pocket rang out. He pulled out the phone only to see who was calling. Again the name read that of his parents. They had called every day since Jack broke the news to them and spent the holiday alone instead of keeping their plans at his parent's home. That was a little over a week ago. He never answered the phone since, unless it was the phone at the office. And even then it was a number known only to his co-workers. His parents probably wanted to make sure he hadn't taken his own life, but the one-liner emails he sent every day reassured them of that. Instead of talking about some amusing thing in the news or event coming up with Ava, all he had now was three words. And he recited them over and over.

*I am fine.*

# Kate Sparrows

Kate Sparrows is a Sassy Sue.

She's a cynical hopeless romantic that's in love with her Kindle and book boyfriends. It's really a love that you shouldn't come between. Well, unless you have ice cream, an awesome accent, or an amazing book in your hand. Bonus points having for all three.

# Acknowledgements

I want to thank Amber Franklin for being my beta reader and for asking for more of Cat's childhood. It forced me to tie up the loose ends and bring the story full circle. I also got to torment Leo and his comic love a bit more.

Ariana from Palimpset Designs – the book cover turned out wonderful. Thank you so much for the revisions we went through and for wanting to make it perfect.

A big thanks to all the people that got behind this book and may have done nothing more than tell one other person.

And most importantly – I want to thank my amazing support network of friends and family. I love you all and I can't begin to thank you enough.

I appreciate all of you more than you'll ever know.

Thank you.

www.ingramcontent.com/pod-product-compliance
Lightning Source LLC
Chambersburg PA
CBHW051953220626
47052CB00004B/920